A BOUQUET

Karel Jaromír Erben

A BOUQUET

of Czech Folktales

*Translated from the Czech
by Marcela Malek Sulak*

Artwork by Alén Diviš

TWISTED SPOON PRESS
PRAGUE • 2020

Translation copyright © 2012 by Marcela Sulak
Illustrations copyright © 2012 by Alén Diviš – Estate
This edition copyright © 2012 by Twisted Spoon Press

*All rights reserved. This book, or parts thereof, may not be used
or reproduced in any form, except in the context of reviews,
without permission in writing from the Publisher.*

ISBN 978-80-86264-41-7
ISBN 978-80-86264-87-5 (e-book)

Contents

List of Illustrations • 7
Translator's Introduction • 9

A Bouquet • 21
The Treasure • 23
Wedding Shirts • 45
Noon Witch • 61
The Golden Spinning Wheel • 66
Christmas Eve • 81
The Dove • 89
Zahor's Bed • 94
Water Sprite • 114
Willow • 129
Lily • 136
A Daughter's Curse • 140
The Prophetess • 143

Author's Notes • 155
About the Author • 171
About the Translator • 172
About the Artist • 173
Acknowledgments • 174

List of Illustrations

FRONTISPIECE
"To the grave the body goes"
1948–49, gouache on paper, 61.5 x 45.7 cm
Museum of the Elbe Region in Poděbrady

PAGE 51
"I'm here! I'm here!"
1948–49), gouache on paper, 37.5 x 26.5 cm
Museum of the Elbe Region in Poděbrady

PAGE 63
"Noon Witch"
1950s, gouache on paper, 63 x 44 cm
Private collection

PAGE 117
"Shine sweet moonlight shine"
1948–49, oil on canvas, 47 x 33.5 cm
The Aleš South Bohemian Gallery

PAGE 128
"But nights her soul sleeps in osiers."
1948–49, gouache on paper, 30 x 24 cm
Private collection

Translator's Introduction

One day in early June 2003 I was sitting in my favorite café in České Budějovice, on a street leading to the Malše River, which surrounds and cradles the old city center as it joins with the Vltava. As I was lifting a tiny wedge of ten-layered *medovník* on a miniature fork, I saw a *vodník*, a water sprite, pass by. All in green, with webbed feet and moss in his hair and across his cheek, he waved at me slyly. We were very close to the water. And beyond the narrow, crooked streets of the old city and the Malše there were thousands of hectares of fishponds dating to 1490, from the time of Vílem of Pernštejn, who had lived just up the Vltava in the original Hluboká Castle. Though momentarily on land, the water sprite was clearly more in his element than I was.

Medovník is almost worth losing one's soul for, but I asked the café owner not to remove the honey cake, and I followed the water sprite to Přemysl Otakar II Square. Apparently, he had agreed to perform in a theater piece about him, and he entered the makeshift stage awaiting him. Before and after the performance, he taunted and gossiped with the inhabitants of the town, who seemed fond, if wary, of him.

Karel Jaromír Erben's *Kytice z pověstí národních* (A Bouquet of Folktales), which contains the ballad "Water Sprite," if "contain" is the most apt verb here, and presents tales of many other popular Czech folk figures, was published in 1853 and expanded in 1861, and it has inspired numerous adaptations ever since. Antonín Dvořák based his four "symphonic poems" on "Water Sprite," "The Dove," "Noon Witch," and "The Golden Spinning Wheel." Jiří Suchý and Ferdinand Havlík's 1972 stage musical of *A Bouquet* is one of the most popular productions in the history of the Semafor Theater, where many Czech stars got their start. In 2001, F.A. Brabec directed the lyrical film *Wildflowers*, using ten of the collection's thirteen tales. At present, Czech television is producing an animated feature using subtitles from my translation of "Christmas Eve." New editions of the collection were printed in 2010 and 2011; in fact, it has never been out of print.

It is said that during the Soviet period the high level of creative and financial investment in the cinematic production of Czech fairy tales was due to the fact that fairy tales were seen as a safe means of expression under a censorious regime. That may be true, but three years after the Velvet Revolution, living and working in the country, I was struck with what felt to me to be a respect for the imagination and for the natural world that we associate with childhood. In fact, I could go into the fields or woods on any given day in any given season with any school child or adult and come home with an armload of delicacies we had gathered on our way: mushrooms, cherries, wild strawberries, blueberries, elderberry flowers (for fritters, syrup, or wine), young nettle for salad or tea, chamomile, St. John's Wort, Mullein. I was introduced to all the sacred trees, the birch groves, the historical lindens, and others. On holidays and weekends I was invited on tours of the countryside to visit castle ruins or palaces restored, as well as ancient sites not listed in any tourist guidebook or found on any map. It might be a stretch to say that the stories of *A Bouquet* are still alive in the countryside, but it is no exaggeration to say that the intimacy with the natural world and its forces, upon which these poems draw, is still very much in evidence.

The Czech literary tradition as we know it – that is, Czech literature written in Czech rather than Latin, Old Church Slavonic, or German – established itself only during the National Revival, which began in the early 19th century. One of the aims of the Revival was the restoration of the Czech language to Bohemia and Moravia after more than two centuries of Germanization under Habsburg rule. Since the people of the countryside had always spoken Czech, unlike those who dwelled in cities and were educated in and conducted their business in German, Erben set about gathering his literary sources from the villages of Bohemia. The thirteen ballads that make up *A Bouquet* establishes a literary depiction of the Czech national character, and, at the same time, links Czech literature to the greater European Romantic movement.

A Bouquet is one of the three foundational texts of Czech literature, and it remains the only one of the three that has not yet been published in English. While my translation fills a scholarly void, it also introduces a beautiful body of literature to anyone who loves folk stories.

"Only those poets are accepted as universal who arrive on

the world scene in their own characteristic — that is, national — costume," observed the Czech writer Jan Neruda. Erben titled his collection *A Bouquet of Folktales*, and this warrants a look into the national characteristic of the narratives he collected. His position as archivist of the National Museum allowed him access to other Slavic folk tales, ancient Greek folk stories, and, of course, the works of the Brothers Grimm, all from which he drew to flesh out his own collection. What is most striking to me is that Erben's tales, in contrast to their German versions, are redemptive. Must all folk heroes suffer? Perhaps — but Erben's heroes suffer for a purpose. Yes, there are forces in the natural world that the heroes cannot control, but unlike the other folk and fairy tales circulating throughout Central Europe at the time, Erben's heroes have inner lives. The forces that tempt and torment them are personal, as well as natural and supernatural. The heroes are rarely stock figures who act only because the plot demands they must. Rather, we see their motives, their aspirations, their temptations.

The characters are universal and national, but they are portrayed here as individuals, as people who have choices and agonize over them. Sometimes they choose wrongly and suffer for it. But sometimes their suffering is not in vain — their inner transformation has won them a reprieve and restored to them what they had lost in the world, or at least it has granted them redemption in the world to come. "Zahor's Bed" shows how steadfast trust in a loving and merciful Christian God can save a soul predestined to hell. Of course, the hero's life on earth is thoroughly consumed in penance and trial, but he never complains of his fate. This story may have had some resonance in Bohemia at the time, a land that was ruled by conquerors, for the plot is set in motion by a father who has sold his son's soul to the devil in exchange for material wealth in this world before the tale begins.

If suffering is a necessary evil, it is only because people refuse to accept their lot in life, or they shirk their responsibilities. Erben apparently assumed people learn by example, so three of the poems are admonishments. In "A Daughter's Curse" and "Noon Witch," poor parenting is punished. One mother lacks the will to discipline, and the other disciplines in anger or frustration. The idea seems to be that faith and industry, familial love, and taking pleasure in the natural world — but not abusing the natural world — will result in salvation, for the individual, the community, and, ultimately, the nation.

Another distinction between the tales Erben collected and their counterparts is the attitude toward labor. In Grimm, labor is often a punishment or a trial, and a good homemaker will often be rewarded by becoming a princess and thus, presumably, never having to work again. In *A Bouquet*, the only domestic chore in which the heroines are engaged (besides preparing dinner for one's husband while trying to placate a temper tantrum — a combination that doesn't end well in "Noon Witch") is spinning.

Since at least the end of the Thirty Years' War, spinning

appears to have been the main industry of a good Czech woman, and Bohemian linen, made from local flax, was considered superior to that from other regions. In a population of fewer than one million at the end of the Thirty Years' War, there were 230,000 flax spinners by 1772. The spinning, of course, was done in the countryside. Only 20% of the population lived in towns, and many of these towns were agrarian in nature. Spinners usually possessed very little land, or none at all. The women in Erben's tales are rewarded for their good spinning: Dora marries a lord, though she is still expected to spin, and she takes pleasure in it. "Christmas Eve" begins and ends with praise for the woman skilled in spinning.

A good spinner is clearly the most virtuous kind of woman. But Czech folk stories rarely present pleasure and labor as mutually exclusive in anyone's life. Spinning will win you your hero, but it will also keep you both happy once you have him. A Czech folktale that Erben did not include, "The Lady in White," features a supernatural spinner who reminds a simple but hardworking shepherdess to enjoy herself. A white-robed lady coaxes Bethushka the shepherdess to leave off her spinning and to dance instead. She rewards Bethushka for her dancing by completing the girl's spinning for her and sending her off with a pouch full of birch leaves that, upon her return home, have turned to gold. The moral of this story seems to be that one should also enjoy life.

Through the years, scholars have read covert nationalistic messages into the poems as well – for example, are the stepmothers and stepsisters representatives of the Habsburg Monarchy who do not love their Czech stepchildren? After all, the stepsister and stepmother in "The Golden Spinning Wheel" do attempt to steal Dora's bridegroom and destiny. The final poem in the collection, "The Prophetess," predicts the rebirth of the Czech nation, but places the blame for its situation squarely on Czech shoulders. The nation's own flaws – its divisiveness, its "wrong-thinking heads" and impure hearts – not the Habsburgs have brought about its downfall. And yet, it would be a mistake to read Erben solely through a political lens, as it would deprive the poems of their human, individual element: the joy of the countryside, even in the midst of poverty, the pain of lost love, the fervent repentance and desire to do better next time, to love more deeply, to appreciate what one has in the moment.

My translation of this important Czech work is sensitive to Erben's prosodic and syntactic innovations that produced a living language filled with the musicality for which Czechs have long been known. I have kept the rhythm and the rhyme scheme, as well as the liquid vowel and consonant combinations, for these poems are, in fact, "songs" – folk songs. I should point out that the rhyme scheme is not always obvious in the original, because it is quite complicated, and there are deviations within the patterns Erben established. I believe the deviations in rhyme are often of narrative significance – that is, they often perform the narrative – so I have kept them.

Many of the poems are written as ballads, with alternating patterns of long and short syllables. Sometimes, though, the total number of syllables is not constant, and for these poems I employed accentual meter in English. In Czech, the length of the syllable is more important than it is in English, which values syllable stress. Accentual verse keeps the number of strongly stressed syllables constant, but varies the unstressed syllables (though slightly). Each line should take the same amount of time to say, unless the line depicts a difficult activity, such as the heroine's flight across the countryside in "Wedding Shirts." Then the combination of consonant sounds will slow the reader down, as will the greater number of strongly stressed syllables. These poems were intended to be read aloud, if not sung, and that is how I have translated them.

I have also been faithful to the meaning and social value of the narrative, and part of this value is allowing the "plain spoken" quality of the work to emerge. Obviously, some of the language of the original is archaic to a Czech ear today, since Czech as a literary language was just being revived at the time of the collection's composition. These small archaic features are evident as well in my use of such expressions as "hark" or "woe is me."

It is undeniably easier to rhyme in Czech than it is in English. Given Czech's seven cases, the sentence structure is relatively flexible compared to that of English. In fact, contemporary Czech poetry often still rhymes. Contemporary English-language poetry usually does not; it is mostly written in free verse. I have avoided violating natural English sentence structure by trying to force or cram the idea into an end-stopped rhyme. I have also refrained from inverting the sentence structure, a practice largely discarded in English-language poetry today, except in greeting cards or light verse. So while I have kept the English sentence as natural as possible, at times I have replaced full rhyme with assonance or consonance (off rhyme or slant rhyme). In some cases I have allowed the sentence or phrase to continue past the line break, creating an enjambment that is not found in the original, and that was not used in English-language poetry contemporaneous to Erben's. I have also taken the occasional liberty of rearranging the order of the lines. These necessary alterations are meant to reproduce the emotional and narrative effects of Erben's original Czech in English.

I have worked on this translation off and on for about fifteen years. During that time, I have acquired many debts and much gratitude. I am grateful to Hana Sedlářová, my first Czech teacher in Zlín, who edited the penultimate version of the manuscript. I am grateful to the entire Sedlářová family, whose hospitality, especially during the holidays, made me feel as if I were a member of the family. Petr Kaláb introduced me to Erben's work and made it come alive to me through our walking and motorcycle tours of the countryside; his friendship has always been the quiet constant that keeps the world magical. Michala and Karel Kudláčkovi, whose home in South Bohemia was always open to me, were helpful in identifying plant species mentioned by Erben. I thank all my students at the Biskupské gymnázium, as well as the patient faculty members. In Israel, Kateřina Zubková, whom I thought I had hired as a baby-sitter, edited the latter half of the translation while my child was napping. I am also grateful to Craig Cravens, who taught me Czech at the University of Texas at Austin and encouraged this project. Most of all, I thank Howard Sidenberg, whose painstaking and intelligent efforts and excellent taste saw this translation through.

Marcela Sulak
Tel Aviv, 2012

A BOUQUET

A Bouquet

Mother died and was laid in her grave,
leaving orphans without her;
every morning they came to the grave,
looking for their mother.

She felt so sad for her son and daughter
her soul crept back one night
and took the form of a tiny flower
which spread across her gravesite.

Now they can smell the breath of their mother,
know that her spirit is with them,
they're glad. And that simple motherful flower
that comforts them they call thyme.

Mother's soul, thyme, from our own dear land,
our folktales are filled with you.
I plucked you from an ancient cairn –
to whom should I carry you?

I will gather you into a modest bouquet
tied with a decorative bow,
travel across the broad land to display you
to family wherever you go.

Maybe some mother's daughter will find you;
your breath will be her sweet perfume.
Maybe you'll come across somebody's son;
his heart will incline to you!

The Treasure

I

Among the beeches on a hill
a little church, its lowly spire;
from the spire the clank of bells
sound through the village and grove nearby.
Not the tone of fine-wrought bells,
but the dark clash of wood on wood,
disappearing in the hills, calls
all to the temple of the Lord.

From the village they come to pray,
rushing out in one big crowd,
pious folk who fear their God,
because today is Good Friday.

The church in mourning: walls are blank,
black cloth covers the altar;
the crucifix is draped in black.
The Passion is sung in the choir.

And look, what is that fair form
through the black woods past the stream?
Some neighboring village woman,

carrying something in her arms.
Flying, oh, she's very quick,
festive in her Sunday best,
across the hill, behind the creek —
in her arms her baby rests.
Running, she descends the hill,
rushes to the temple of the Lord;
there, on the side near the forest slope,
the church sits on the little hill.
And in the valley at the creek
suddenly she's twice as fleet:
and like the wind that's blown and stirred,
the sound of song is ringing
from the church, the choir is singing
the Passion of Christ the Lord.
Running, running down the rocks:
"What's this? Have my eyes grown weak?
Can I believe them?" She balks,
glances around bewildered —
stepping quickly she backtracks,
stops again, and now turns back —
"Here's the brush and there's the wood,
and the path across the field —
I couldn't have lost the road!
God, what's happening to me!
Don't I stand before a stone,
but changed into a different one?"

Again she stops, again hurries,
strangest thing she's ever known,
rubbing her eyes with her fists,
stepping forth in starts and fits,
"God, it's changed! Not the same one!"

Three hundred steps from the church
in the middle of the road,
what appears now through the brush,
where once a large stone stood?
An entrance to a gaping hole
appears before the woman now,
the stone stands in the road —
how to explain it? She doesn't know —
but an entire cliff has sprung
as if from when time first began
it had stood. A new corridor
opens beneath the earth for her;
swollen with sparkling quartz,
and where the chamber disappears
in the hill's dark lap there burns
a flame, brightly pale, it flickers,
glowing pale, luminescent
like the moon shines in the night,
then like the sun as it sets,
it's flooded in ruddy light.

And the woman marvels at the sight,
moves to enter the galleries,
lifts her hand to shield her eyes
because the place is very bright.
"God, how it's shining with light!"
She rubs her eyes with her hands,
and step by step she advances.
"What light, what strange, strange light!
What could it be? What might . . ."
Scared to advance any more,
she gazes at the corridor.

And so she stands and hesitates,
her eyes locked on the chamber;
her fear leaves her as she stares,
curiosity compels her,
and the woman enters deeper.
Step by step, deeper and deeper,
she's powerfully compelled to go,
step by step, into the boulder,
until she wakes a sleeping echo.
And the deeper the woman goes,
the greater grows the strange light.
Nearing now the chamber's end,
she's grown so dazzled and so
dazed, she can't bear the direct light,
and she covers her face with her hand.

She sees, she sees — oh, what she sees,
who among the people has seen?
Such beauty, such luster and shine
is possible only in heaven!

Doors open on a marvelous
salon; its walls fashioned
of gold, they are luminous,
the ruby ceiling, lustrous,
lifted on crystal columns.
On either side of the door —
who's not seen would call her liar —
for across the marble floor,
two fires flicker, two fires
flicker on the marble floor;
nothing can put out these fires.
On the left, above the silver side,
the fires leap toward the moon;
above the gold fire on the right,
the bright sun will always shine.
The fire burns, and the room shines,
wrapped in its own bright light;
as long as the treasure remains,
nothing will quench the flaming light
nor overwhelm its luster.

The woman stands at the threshold;
she stands blinded by the gleam,
not lifting her eyes; she's not bold
enough to look at the flame.
Holding the child in her left hand,
with her right she rubs her eyes,
then she musters self-command,
recovers herself on the whole;
she ponders her life with great sighs
and begins to speak with her soul:
"Dear God, what a time I've had! My share
of hunger and poverty!
This place is filled with such treasure,
but I've always lived wretchedly!
Silver and gold, and so much,
quite a stash here underground;
just a fistful from that pile
would make me very rich.
We'd be happy from now on,
me and my little child!"

And as she stands and thinks,
she's more tempted by desire;
arming herself with a crucifix,
she approaches the pale fire.
She takes a piece of silver, lifts
it, and puts it back again;

lifts it, considers it again,
its luster and weight; should she abstain —
should she put it back again?
No, it's in her lap — it slipped.
And emboldened by this success:
"Surely it was God's own hand
that brought us to this treasure place,
because he wants me to be blessed:
it would be a sin if I'd attempt
to hold his blessing in contempt!"

That's what the woman tells herself,
setting the little boy down.
Spreading her apron, she kneels,
hungrily gathering from the piles,
piling the silver in her lap:
"Surely this is God's own hand,
who wants us rich and happy!"
She keeps taking from the pile —
her lap full, she can hardly stand.
She's tucked some into her hair band,
the silver's so beguiling!
And now she's ready to go,
oh, and here's that little knave!
How to take him with her load?
He's two years old, this little knave;
but throwing happiness away

seems to her a bad idea.
And yet she can't take both.

Look! – his mother takes the silver!
The child begins to tremble for her:
"Mama! Mama, Mama!" he screeches;
with his little hands he clutches.
"Hush, hush, my little boy, my son,
just wait right here, I'll not be gone
a minute, Mama's coming back!"

She's running, running through the chamber
till she's left it quite behind her;
along the hill, across the creek,
to the woods on joyful feet;
in a little while she hastens
back again, empty and free,
scarcely able to breathe,
she returns to her destination.

And like the wind that's softly heard,
the sound of song is ringing
from the church, the choir is singing
the Passion of Christ the Lord.

As she hurries to the chamber –
"Ha ha, Mama, ha ha, Mama!"

laughs the child with joy; he clambers,
clapping his hands for his mama.

But Mother pays him no attention,
shining metal moves her more —
and gold is what she most adores.
To the opposite direction,
spreading her apron, she kneels,
hungrily gathering from the piles,
piling the gold in her lap.
Her lap is so full she can hardly stand —
she's tucked some into her hair band!
She's full of her own happiness,
oh but how her heart leaps!

When his mother starts to carry
the gold, the child trembles for her,
trembles in despair and weeps,
"Mama! Mama, Mama!" he screeches;
with his little hands he clutches.
"Hush, hush, my little boy, my son,
just wait right here, I'll not be gone
a minute, Mama's coming back!"
Reaching her hand to her lap,
she lifts out two bright coins,
then she leans toward her son,
clinks them together, tap tap:

"Look at your mama, and see
what she has and how it clinks?"
But he continues to weep —
though she's so happy her heart leaps.

Again she tucks into her lap, pulls
more gold out, this time a fistful,
lays it in the child's lap — "Just see
what Mama gives you, hush baby!
Hush, my boy, hush, hush my son:
clink-clink, hear how it rings?
Wait a while, I won't be gone
for long. Mama will back, you'll see.
Play my, child, play nicely. That's it,
wait just a while, just wait a bit."

Running, running through the chamber
till she's left it quite behind her,
doesn't look back at her dear,
and now the creek is drawing near
along the hill, across the creek,
to the woods with her gold, on joyful feet.
At her hut, looking it over:

"Ha, my hut, you plain, old shack,
you'll be standing lonesome here!
Now what's there to hold me back?

Nothing in you was ever dear
to me. I'll go away from this
dark forest, Father's shabby roof;
happiness lies somewhere else,
home for me is elsewhere, too!
I'm leaving this region; my feet
can't wait to find the road, they're giddy.
I'm leaving, my joy is complete;
I'm going to the big city.
I'll buy castles and land there,
they'll treat me like a lady, then.
Shabby little hut of mine, fare
well. I won't live in you again!
No poor widow anymore,
heavy burdens day and night:
Look in my lap" – and at that word,
she glances there with great delight. –
Oh, if only she hadn't looked there!
Now she's turning pale in fear;
she's nearly fainting on the spot,
collapsing to the ground in fright.
Sees, she sees, ha! what she sees,
she herself hardly believes!
She breaks the weathered doors, she heaves
herself onto the chest that hoards
all her precious silver stores,
pushes back the lid – ha, what she sees

would test anyone's belief,
oh, what another shock! Instead
of silver there is only stone,
and in her apron, the scarf from her head,
horrible incomprehension,
instead of gold only clay!
And all her hope is crushed! – –

Unworthy of happiness,
not understanding she'd been blessed.

II

When she's crushed and torn apart,
once this loss is understood,
something pierces her womanly heart;
she screams with horror pure and stark;
she screams so that her hut is shook:
"Oh my child, my child, my dear!
Dear child – my dear – oh my dear!"
These words ring through the deep wood.

And with terrible apprehension
she runs – oh, she doesn't run, she flies;
she flies like a bird, she flies
through the woods, across the hillside

to where she found her fortune,
on the hill where the church lies.

From the church a light wind stirs,
you don't hear singing anymore?
The Passion of Christ the Lord
is no longer sung in the choir.

When she arrives at the chamber,
ha, and what a sight greets her!
Three hundred steps from the church
in the middle of the road
no corridor appears through the brush,
where once a large stone stood!
Even the cliff disappeared
as if it had never stood.

Ah, this woman, how appalled,
how she speeds across the hill,
how she dreads, and seeks and calls
through the brush, she's deathly pale!
Oh the mouth, white as a corpse,
desperation in her eyes! See
her tear across the unkempt copse
dashing toward the valley!
"Woe, woe is me! It isn't here!"
Her skin is ripped by brush and torn,

her feet are pierced through by thorns —
all for naught, it's very clear,
the entrance simply isn't there!

She falls once more into despair,
anxiety grips her anew:
"Who will give me back my child, who?
Oh, my child, where are you? Where?!"

"Here, deep underground am I,"
whispers a voice carried by wind,
"you can't see me with your eye,
no ear will ever comprehend!

"Peace, peace below the earth, so pure,
nothing to eat, nothing to drink,
lying on the marble floor,
with pure gold in my lap to clink!

"Night and day don't alternate;
I never sleep, don't close my eyes,
playing nicely, how I play —
clink-clink! hear how it chimes?"

She looks again to no avail;
anxiety grips her anew:
she flings herself down, wretched,

tearing her hair from her head,
bloody and deathly pale:

"Oh, woe is me! Woe, woe!
Oh, my child, where are you? where?
Where can I find you, my child, my dear?!
Dearest child – my dear – my dear!"
These words ring through the forest.

III

One day passes, then another,
and days into weeks; weeks turn
into a month, then summer
starts up and begins to burn.

Among the beeches on a hill,
a little church, its lowly spire;
from day to day the church bells peal
through the village and grove nearby.
Here, above, in the morning when
the bells ring out for matins
a pious peasant bows and leans
her brow on the tabernacle.

Does anyone know this woman,
whose brow is bowed to the ground?
The candles have long burned out
at the altar, but she kneels on.
She doesn't even seem to breathe –
her cheeks and lips are very pale –
oh, she prays so quietly!
Who is it? I can't really tell,
but I could guess. When, after Mass
is done and the church door is closed,
you can see her, through the beeches pass,
taking her leave of the hill. She goes
taking the path, somber and slow,
through the brush where one great stone
juts to the middle of the road
from among the rocks. She moans
each time she gets there and sighs
and presses her forehead to her
palm, "Oh my child," and her eyes
are filling and flowing with tears.

Unhappy woman from the hut,
always sad and always pallid,
always, always deep in thought:
from early morning to late night
her eyes are never touched with light;
every night her sleep is hid

in grief. And when each morning
she rises from her troubled bed,
"Oh woe is me, oh woe is me,
oh, my child, my child, dear child!
Forgive me, oh merciful God!"

Fall and winter have passed away,
it's now gone, the entire year —
her grief's as heavy as the first day,
her eyes haven't shed all their tears.
And when the sun rose high in the sky
and warmed the earth again to spring,
it couldn't coax the mouth to smile;
the widow is still weeping.

IV

Listen! Above the beeches on the hill,
from the little church, its lowly spire,
you can hear the church bells peal
through the village and grove nearby.
And look! to Mass they make their way,
rushing out in one big crowd,
pious folk who fear their God,
because today is Good Friday.

Breezes blowing soft as spring,
and from the tower song is heard:
once more in the church they sing
the Passion of Christ the Lord.

A woman moves across the slope,
from the forest to the creek.
What is it makes her movement slow?
The memory of a year ago
this day weights her steps with grief!
Closer, closer, she approaches,
only now she's where the rock is.

And look, what appears through the brush?
In the middle of the road,
three hundred steps from the church,
where once a large stone stood,
the entrance to a gaping hole;
the stone stands in the road,
but an entire cliff has sprung
as if it stood since time began.

And she's horrified at the sight;
her hair stands up in terror:
the weight of her grief hits her
and the weight of her guilt. And though
she's afraid, she doesn't hesitate —

she bounds in her dread and her hope
across the familiar corridor,
the corridor beneath the rock wall.

And look, a marvelous
salon; its walls fashioned
of gold, they are luminous,
the ruby ceiling, lustrous,
lifted on crystal columns.
On either side of the door
across on the marble floor
flicker, flicker two fires.
On the left, above the silver side
the fires leap toward the moon;
above the gold on the right,
the bright sun will always shine.

And in awe the woman draws near,
probing the room with wide eyes
in her hope and in her fear.
Do silver and gold attract her?
Oh, she doesn't care anymore! —
"Ha ha, Mama! ha, ha, Mama!"
Oh, it's her child, it's the child
that she mourned the entire year,
clapping his little hands!

But the woman can't even breathe,
she is trembling in wonder,
and with frantic alacrity
she clasps the child in her arms
and sweeps him across the long hall.

And crash, crash! bang! it roars
from the base of the hill at her heels;
a terrific crack, the wind snarls;
earth quakes in chaotic thunder –
the chamber collapses at her heels!
"Mother of God, help me, Mother!"
cries the woman anxiously;
she turns, afraid of what she'll see.

And look! Again, what a change!
All's silent; now a great stone
juts in the middle of the road
from the brush; everything's as before,
no trace of a corridor:
they've finished singing in the choir
the Passion of Christ the Lord.

The woman can't even breathe,
she is trembling in wonder,
and with frantic alacrity
she is lifting her child to her,

pressing him against her breast
as if she were afraid for him;
she runs, without breath or rest
until the rock's far behind them.
She runs without once looking back,
in her joy and in her fear
across the slope till she's near
the trees, at the poor forest shack.

Oh, how the woman thanks her God
with fervent sincerity!
Look at how the tears still drop,
how she embraces her child,
presses him to her repeatedly,
kissing his forehead, his hands, little lips;
she's simply floating in delight!

Look, what's that sparkle in her lap?
What's that ringing sound? – Pure gold!
Gold she gave to her child
in the cave last year when she told
him to be good and play a while.

It has caused her so much sorrow,
it no longer moves the widow.
It cost her so many tears!
She thanks God anyway, though,

longingly pressing her precious child!
She knows from bitter experience,
it's not much, the glitter of gold,
but nothing's worth more than a child!

    V

The church was pulled down long ago,
clanging bells no longer sound;
there, where the beeches used to blow,
a rotting roof litters the ground.

But an old man remembers a lot;
though many graves have since appeared,
people will still point it out,
once long ago, that place was here.

And in the frosty evenings when
the young folks sit and gather,
the old man likes to tell them
of the widow and the treasure.

Wedding Shirts

Eleven o'clock has come and gone,
and still a lamp is shining on,
and still a lamp is burning there,
suspended over a kneeler.

On the wall of the lowly room,
like a bud and a rose in bloom,
was the holy family hung,
the parents of God and their son.

Before the image of those three,
a young girl prays on bended knee:
her head is bowed her hands are crossed,
her hands are crossed over her breast;
tears are streaming from her eyes,
her chest is heaving, then she sighs.
And when a hovering tear drops down,
it falls upon her soft white gown.

"Oh dear God, where is my daddy?
Grass is growing on his body!
Oh dear God, where is my mother?
There she lies – next to my father!

My sister didn't live a year;
a bullet killed my brother.

"I'm so unhappy; once I had
a lover, but he's gone abroad
and still has not returned. And I
would have given him my life.

"Before he left he dried my eyes,
comforted me with his advice:
'Sow flax, my dear, sow flax in May,
say you'll think of me each day.
Mind the spinning that first year,
then wet the cloth beside the weir,
stitch the shirts in the third year:
when the sewing is complete,
weave some flowers into a wreath.'

"I've sewn the shirts and done my best;
I've stored them in a wooden chest.
The flowers now have dried and curled,
my love still wanders through the world,
the wide, wide world; he's lost and free,
like a stone in the deep sea.
Three years without a word of news,
does he live, is he well? Only God knows.

"Oh mighty Virgin Mary,
give me strength, oh please help me:
If my lover's lost in foreign charms,
bring him back into my arms –
he's the only flower I have left –
give him back, or give me death.
With him the world is spring in bloom,
without him all is winter gloom.
Loving mother, dear Mary,
help me now in all my grief!"

The picture on the wall then stirs –
the young girl screams in terror;
the lamp which threw dim rays about
sputters once and then goes out.
Perhaps it was a draft of wind –
or else an evil omen!

Listen, on the porch a step,
and at the window: tap, tap, tap!
". . . Are you sleeping or awake, my dear?
Hey, my doll, I'm here! I'm here!
Hey, my doll, how are you?
Have you remembered? Are you true?
Or does another love you?"

"Oh, my love! Thank God, my dear!
I was thinking of you now at prayer.
At this time I think of you
and say a prayer here at this pew!"

"Ha, stop praying and let's go —
I will lead and you follow.
The moon will light our way tonight,
for I've returned to claim my bride."

"What are you saying? For God's sake!
Where would we go now? It's so late!
The wind is roaring; anyway,
it's almost daylight, come let's wait."

"Oh, night is day, and day is night —
by day a dream presses my eyes!
Before the roosters are awake,
you'll be my bride, the bride I'll take.
Don't hesitate, rise up and come —
I must take you, make you my own."

The darkness is profound that night,
from the heights the moon shines bright,
desolate and silent village,
nothing there but the wind's wild rage.

He goes before her – leap by leap –
she follows after, step by step.
The village dogs begin to howl
as when they smell something foul
or strange, like strangers on the fly,
or when they sense a corpse nearby!

"Clear, beautiful night – I've heard it said
it's the time graves open and the dead
could be closer than you think – my dear,
does that thought cause you any fear?"

"Why should I be afraid? You're with me
and God's eye is above me. –
But tell me, my dear, do tell,
is your father alive and well?
Your dear father, and your mother,
will she be as glad as I to meet her?"

"Too many questions, doll, for me,
just come quickly – you will see.
Let's get going – time won't wait,
our journey is a long one yet.
But what's that in your right hand, dear?"

"I'm carrying some books of prayer."

"Throw them out, those kind of books
are heavier than piles of rocks!
Throw them out and walk with ease,
if you want to keep up with me."

He takes and tosses them to the side,
then leaps with her a good ten miles.

And their way winds through the highlands,
desolate forest and craggy sands,
through gorges and over cliffs,
and wild bitches bark and sniff,
and all the birds broadcast the news
that unhappiness draws close.

And he always before her – leap by leap –
she follows after, step by step.
Among the rosehips where stones glint,
beside the hawthorns, over flint;
everywhere the white feet move,
there remain traces of blood.

"Clear, beautiful night – I've heard it said
it's the time when the living walk with the dead;
the dead could be closer than you think – my dear,
does that thought cause you any fear?"

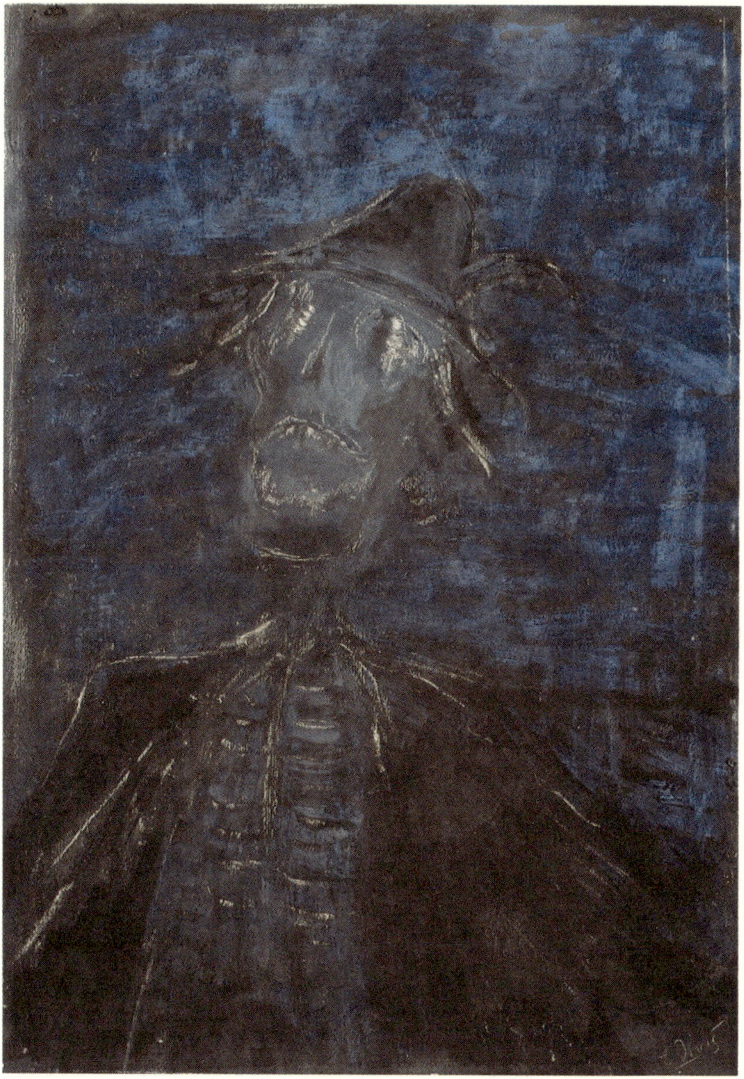

"Why should I be afraid? You're with me,
and God's hand is above me. —
But tell me, tell me only this,
what is it like, I mean, your house?
Is it tidy, full of cheer?
Perhaps there is a chapel near?"

"Too many questions, doll, for me!
Just come quickly — you will see.
Let's get going — time won't wait,
our journey is a long one yet.
But what's that round your waist I see?"

"I brought my rosary with me."

"Ha, a rosary made of bladdernut
will squeeze you thin and snake about
your chest till you can't breathe at all:
throw it out — don't let us stall."

He takes and tosses it to the side,
then leaps with her some twenty miles.

And their path moves down the lowlands,
across water, meadows, fens,
and in the swamps and in the cane,
blue lights flicker off and on:

they form two rows with nine in each,
as when a body's laid to rest.
From the stream the frogs emerge,
croaking out a funeral dirge.

And he always before her – leap by leap –
she follows after, step by step.
Razor-sharp, the grass blades cut
the poor girl's white and tender feet.
And the green fern's furling frond
is colored red with her fresh blood.

"Clear, beautiful night – I've heard it said
it's the time when the living rush to the grave;
the dead could be closer than you think – my dear,
does that thought cause you any fear?"

"Oh, I'm not afraid while you're with me,
and the Lord's will is over me. –
But give me just a little rest,
it feels like knives stab at my chest.
Don't hurry so, my spirit's wan,
my knees are weak, I can't go on."

"Hurry, my girl, come, now come,
now we'll be there very soon.
The guest are waiting, and the feast

and time flies like a bullet, fast.
What's that you've pinned to the lace
on the collar of your nightdress?"

"My mother gave me her crucifix."

"Ha that damned gold has a jagged edge;
it's cut you, now look how you've bled!
And it hurts me even more.
Take it off, my bird, and soar!"

He takes and tosses it to the side,
then leaps with her some thirty miles.

A building rises from the wide plane,
tall with long and narrow panes,
and rising high above roof tiles,
a bell tower and a spire.

"Hey, my doll, we're finally here.
Can you see anything, my dear?"

"Oh God, do you mean that church?"

"It's my castle, not a church!"

"The row of crosses – a graveyard?"

"Those aren't crosses, that's my orchard!
Hey, look at me, my doll,
and leap with joy over the wall!"

"Oh, go away, leave me in peace!
How horrid, savage is your face;
oh, your breath smells dangerous,
and your heart's an icy crust."

"There's nothing at all, my love, to fear!
We've got plenty in my castle here:
Though without blood, there's lots of meat —
oh, but today it's different, what a treat!
What's that in your bundle, my dear?"

"All the shirts I've sewn these years."

"We don't need many, only two:
The first for me, the next for you."

He lifts the bundle with a laughing grin,
tosses it on the grave beyond the fence.
"Fear not, follow me, my doll,
leap after the bundle over the wall!"

"But you've always gone ahead,
and I've been following your lead

on this hard journey. You go before.
You jump first; I'll follow once more!"

And so he leaps across the wall,
never expecting her betrayal.
He leaps five yards into the air,
but he cannot not see her anywhere:
just the whiteness of her dress
reveals the speed of her egress.
Her coffin, true, is very near —
but he never expected this from her!

There a little chamber stands:
the door is low against her hands.
The young girl's safety is the latch,
and then it closes — hear it catch.
A simple building, no windows; tonight
the moon shines through it like twilight.
The solid building is a morgue —
inside a corpse lies on a board.

Outside the noise is growing loud,
graveyard ghouls in a mighty crowd
murmur and clatter, pace and throng,
shrieking out this dreadful song:

"To the grave the body goes,

but woe to any who neglect the soul!"

And at the door now: knock, knock knock!
Outside her spouse roars, "lift the lock!
Rise up, you corpse, arise,
and move the latch aside!"

And now the dead opens its eyes,
and now it rubs its deadened eyes,
collects itself, raises its head
and looks around from side to side.

"Holy God, aid me: if You command,
I will remain in the devil's hand! –
Lie down, dead man, and don't arise,
and may God grant you eternal peace!"

The dead man then lays down his head
and shuts his eyes, is once more dead. –

And once more: knock, knock knock!
Cries louder still, "lift the lock!
Arise, you corpse, be limber
and open up the chamber!"

And when he hears that voice, that tone,
he lifts once more his flesh and bone

and aims his stiff shoulder
toward the latch there at the door.

"Save my soul, oh Jesus Christ,
have mercy, by your sacrifice! —
Lie down, you dead, lie and be still;
God grant you peace, and me as well!"

The dead man then lays down his head,
extends his limbs, is once more dead. —

And once again: Knock, knock, knock!
"Get up you corpse, open the lock,
and pass the living to me here!"
The young girl cannot see or hear.

Oh woeful girl, to her dismay,
the dead man rises, turns her way
for the third time; his large, cloudy eyes
turn on the girl half-dead with fright.

"Virgin Mary, be with me,
and please pray to your son for me!
I beg you, unworthy as I am:
Oh, forgive me and forgive my sin!
Rescue me, Mary, loving mother,
save me from that evil power."

Listen, from the next town over,
a rooster crows and then another,
and then another in the village,
all roosters crow and shake their plumage. —

The dead, as soon as he has stood,
collapses again onto the board.
The horde outside has disappeared,
and the evil spouse, no sound is heard.

In the morning, on their way to Mass,
people crowd around amazed.
One empty tomb stands on its head,
there's a girl in the chamber with the dead,
and thrown over every gravestone
shredded shirts, each newly sewn. —

Young maiden, it was good you thought
to turn and ask for help from God
and to have left your evil spouse.
Had you chosen a different course
things would have ended much worse.
And your body, lovely, white,
would have ended like these shirts.

Noon Witch

A child stands crying at his bench,
shrieking as loud as he could.
"If only you'd be quiet! Hush,
you gypsy! and be good!

"Your papa's coming home at noon
and won't like waiting for his food.
The fire's too low, will be out soon
because of troublesome you!

"Hush, here's a wagon and a rooster –
play with your soldier – he'll be a guard!"
But wagon, soldier, rooster
fly – bang! – into the corner, hard.

Then piercing screams arise anew.
"I wish a hornet . . . you are so wild . . .
I'll call the noon witch on you,
you ungovernable child!

"Come and get him, noon witch, come
take him! I can bear no more!"
And look, someone's outside – a thumb
is stealthily working the lock at the door.

A wild, thin face, small and brown,
is hid beneath a wrinkled veil,
a crutch, bent shanks, menacing frown,
such a voice — like a maddened gale!

"Give me the child!" — "Oh Lord, oh Christ!
Forgive the sinner her sin!"
But death is near and breathing close
at the sight of the noon witch's grin.

At the table creeping quietly,
a shadow, the witch, with fingers spread.
Mama now can scarcely breathe,
clutching the child with arms of lead.

Her arms around him, she looks back, wild.
The noon witch creeps up even nearer —
woe, woe to the little child —
the noon witch is almost here!

Now the noon witch's hands are reaching
as the mother's shoulders clench,
"for the sake of Christ's dear suffering" —
she falls to the floor without sense.

Now listen — one, two, three, four . . .
the bell is striking noon.

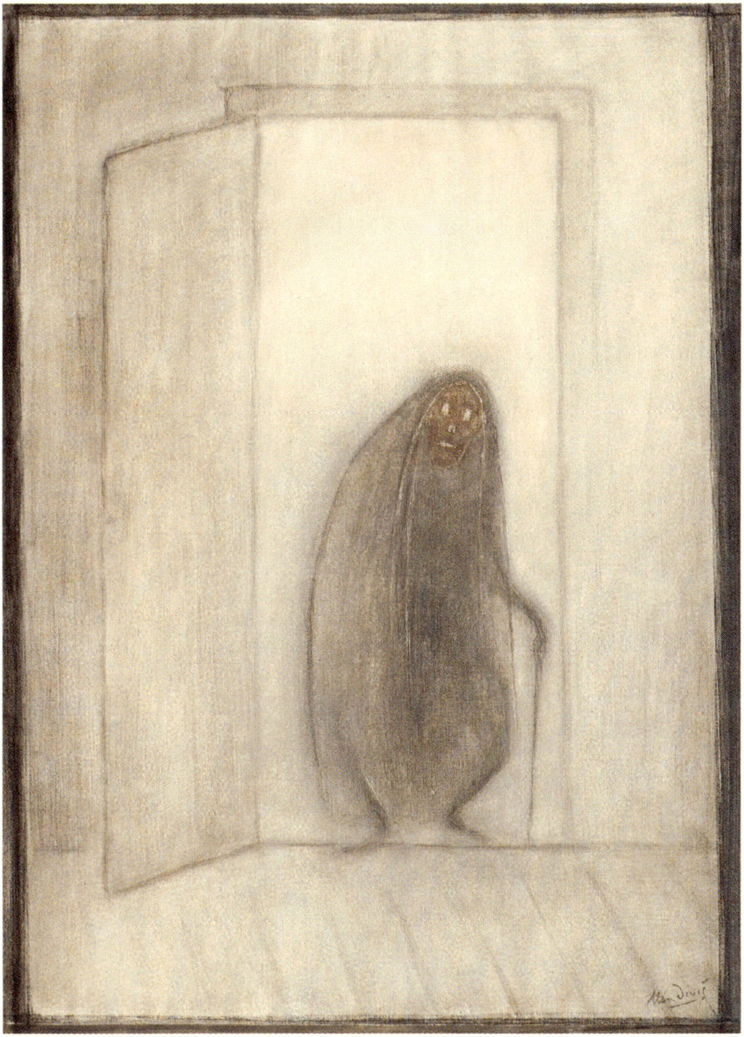

The handle turns, and through the door
Papa strides into the room.

Mama's fallen by the door;
the child rises and falls on her breath.
As Papa lifts her from the floor
he sees the child — squeezed to death.

The Golden Spinning Wheel

I

Around the wood a sprawling field,
a lord comes riding from the wood,
he rides a fine black fiery steed,
how merrily its horseshoes ring.
He rides alone.

The steed is at the cottage: hop!
And on that cottage door: rap rap!
"Open the door to me, hey, hey!
pursuing game I lost my way,
Bring me some water!"

Out comes a girl like a flower,
from the well she draws him water;
he's never seen in all his life
such a beauty. She sits at her distaff
spinning, spinning flax.

The lord is standing, not knowing what
he wanted; he's even forgot
his great thirst. He sees the slender,
even thread. He can't take his eyes off her,
the pretty spinner.

"Give me your hand, if you are free,
you must become my wife!" And he
pulls her to him by her hips.
"Oh sir, I have no will except
that of my mother."

"And where, girl, is your mother?
I don't see anyone else here." —
"Oh, sir, she is my stepmother,
she's in the city with her daughter,
they come tomorrow."

II

Around the wood a sprawling field,
once more the lord rides from the wood,
he rides a fine black fiery steed,
how merrily its horseshoes ring,
straight to the cottage.

The steed is at the cottage: hop!
And on that cottage door: rap rap!
"Dear people, open the door to me!
that my eyes will once more see
my only pleasure!"

All skin and bone, a crone steps out,
"Ho, what has our noble guest brought?"
"I bring you change, I'll change your life,
I want your daughter for my wife —
stepdaughter, I mean."

"Will wonders never cease, lordling?
Who could imagine such a thing?
You're very welcome, noble guest,
but tell me, sir, how came you to us?
I don't know your name."

"I am the king, lord of the land,
I stopped here yesterday by chance:
I'll give you gold, I'll give you silver,
in exchange, give me your daughter,
the pretty spinner."

"Will wonders never cease, oh King!
Who could imagine such a thing?
We are not worthy, good sir King,
we do not merit anything
but for your mercy.

"But heed my counsel: take my daughter,
not the step one — my own daughter.
Like two eyes in a single head,

they're just alike, and — oh, her thread —
her thread is like silk!"

"Old crone, that's terrible advice,
do what I say, that will suffice:
tomorrow at the break of day
escort your stepchild on her way
to the king's castle!"

III

"Wake up, daughter, now it's time,
the king awaits with feasting, wine:
I wasn't expecting this, it's true —
may everything go well for you
in the king's castle!"

"Get dressed, get dressed, oh sister, mine,
the royal castle will be fun:
You've aimed so high that I can't follow,
see how you've left me here below —
well, I wish you health!"

"Come, come, Dora, don't be late,
let's not make your husband wait;
before you even reach the woods

you'll forget your home, now mark my words —
come on, hurry up!"

"Mother, I don't understand,
why the knife there in your hand?" —
"A knife is handy in the shade
for jabbing eyes of evil snakes —
come on, hurry up!"

"Sister, I don't understand,
why the axe there in your hand?" —
"An axe is good if we need to hack
the limbs of beasts should they attack —
come on, hurry up!"

As soon as they reach the wood's cool shade:
"Ha, you are the beast; you are the snake!"
Hill and dale cry out against
the murder of this maid. The violence
wrought by two women!

"Now take your pleasure with the king,
his agile body, anything
you want, embrace him fresh in bed,
regard his calm, unlined forehead,
my pretty spinner!" —

"Mama, what to do with these,
where to put the limbs and eyes?" —
"Don't leave them with the body, daughter,
someone might put them back together —
best take them with you."

And when they leave the evergreens:
"Don't worry about anything,
for you are just alike, it's said,
as two eyes in a single head —
don't worry at all!"

The king looks out the window and
sees them approach, gathers his men;
he meets them on the road, his bride
and her mother. And their lie
goes undetected.

And the wedding completes the crime,
the maiden bride laughs all the time;
there is feasting without measure,
music, dancing, every pleasure,
a full seven days.

But at the dawning of the eighth,
the king and soldiers go away:
"Farewell, my lady, I must go

to wage cruel war against a foe.
I am leaving now.

"If I return from war alive,
we'll renew the flower of our love.
Remember me, be true until.
Spin diligently at the wheel,
spin plenty of thread!"

    IV

And now, what's happened to the maid,
deep in the thicket where she's lain?
Six open wounds have poured their blood,
have turned into a living flood
that fed the green moss.

A sudden change in circumstance,
the body's cold, the blood is stanched –
and now's her awful deadly night.
Cursed the moment the king caught sight
of her, cursed, cursed!

And then a strange old man appears
from the forest rocks. A silver beard
falls all the way down to his knees.

Onto his shoulder he lifts the body,
brings it to a cave.

"Get up my servant, run and sell —
be quick — this golden spinning wheel.
Sell it in the royal castle,
don't take any pay, my vassal,
but ask for two legs." —

The servant sits at the gate just so;
the queen looks out of her window,
sees his golden spinning wheel,
"if only I had that spinning wheel
fashioned of pure gold!

"Rise up Mother, you'd do me well
to see what he wants for the spinning wheel." —
"Buy it, lady, it's not very dear,
my father doesn't value it much. Here,
have it for two legs."

"For legs? Oh my, how very strange!
But I must have it anyway.
Go, Mama, to the chamber
and take the two legs of our Dora,
and give them to him."

And with the legs the servant returns
to the forest: "Sir, it's done." –
"Fetch me living water, my boy;
cleanse the body, make it whole,
whole as it once was."

He touches each wound then with water,
and the legs receive life's fire:
the body grows whole again,
as whole as it has ever been,
without a blemish.

"Jump to it boy, run and fetch
that golden distaff from the shelf:
Sell it in the royal castle,
don't take any pay, my vassal,
but ask for two hands!" –

The servant sits at the gate just so;
the queen looks out of her window,
and when she sees his golden distaff,
"if only I had that distaff
for the spinning wheel!

"Mother, dearest, oh my life,
see what he wants for that distaff." –
"Buy it, lady, it's not very dear,

my father doesn't value it much. Here,
have it for two hands."

"Two hands? Oh my, how very strange!
But I must have it anyway.
Go, Mama, to the chamber
and take the two hands of our Dora,
and give them to him."

And with the hands the servant returns
to the forest: "Sir, it's done." —
"Fetch me living water, my boy;
cleanse the body, make it whole,
whole as it once was."

He touches each wound then with water,
and the hands receive life's fire:
the body grows whole again,
as whole as it has ever been,
without a blemish.

"Jump to it, lad, be on your way
and sell that golden cone today:
Sell it in the royal castle,
don't take any pay, my vassal,
but ask for two eyes." —

The servant sits at the gate just so;
the queen looks out of her window,
and when she sees his golden cone,
"if only I had that cone
for the gold distaff!

"Rise up, Mama, go once more,
ask what he's selling that cone for." –
"Buy it, lady, it's not very dear,
my father doesn't value it much. Here,
have it for two eyes."

"For eyes?! But that's unheard of boy!
Who is your father anyhow?"
"It does no good to know his name,
if you look for him he won't be found,
he must come himself."–

"Mother, Mama, what should I do?
I must have that gold cone, too!
Go once more to the chamber
and take the eyes of our Dora,
and give them to him."

And with the eyes the servant returns
to the forest: "Sir, it's done." –
"Fetch me living water, my boy;

cleanse the body, make it whole,
whole as it once was."

He lays the eyes in their sockets,
and their fire's reignited.
And the maiden looks around
without seeing anyone,
no one but herself.

V

The battle ends the third Sunday,
the king rides happily away:
"And how are you, my dear lady,
were you mindful," he asks gaily,
"of my final words?"

"Oh, I've taken them to heart,
for love of you, see what I bought:
my spinning wheel, and its own cone
and distaff, made from solid gold,
each one of a kind!"

"Come sit, my lady, go ahead,
for love of me spin golden thread." –
She sits down, eager, at the wheel,

but as it turns she grows quite pale —
what misery — a song!

"Whirrr — evil is the thread you spin!
You came here to beguile the king:
You killed your own stepsister, then
picked out her eyes, hacked off her limbs —
whirrr — that evil thread!"

"Is that a spinning wheel you're playing?
I'm not sure what those words are saying!
The way you play is so bizarre,
my lady, play for me some more:
carry on, lady!"

"Whirrr — evil is the thread you spin!
You wanted to beguile the king:
And so you killed the king's true bride,
then you yourself became the bride —
whirrr — that evil thread!"

"Oh, how horribly you play!
You aren't as you appear, lady!
Play a third time as before
so I might hear even more:
carry on, lady!"

"Whirrr — evil is the thread you spin!
You came here to beguile the king:
You hid your sister in forest stones
then took her husband for your own —
whirrr — that evil thread!"

At these words, he mounts his horse
and rides it deep into the forest;
he searches, calling through the wood:
"Where are you, my Dora, my beloved,
where are you, beloved?" —

VI

Around the wood a sprawling field
from the wood a lord and a lady ride,
they ride a fine, black fiery steed,
how merrily the horseshoes ring,
toward the castle.

A second wedding has occurred,
a blooming flower, the maiden bride;
there was feasting without measure,
music, dancing, every pleasure,
it lasted three weeks.

And what about the crone, the mother?
And what about the snake, the daughter? —
Oh, four wolves hunt in the forest,
each carrying a leg he's foraged
from two women's bodies.

What they'd done to the first maid —
the eyes extracted from the head,
limbs hacked off — they were condemned
to have the same thing done to them
in the thick forest.

What of the golden spinning wheel?
What kind of song will it play now? — Well,
it sang three times, then disappeared,
and no one ever saw or heard
the spinning wheel again.

Christmas Eve

I

Frost blows at the window, dark as the grave;
in the room it's warm by the stove;
an old woman dreams in the fire's glow,
girls spinning linen as she dozes.

"Spinning wheel, you whir and spin,
soon, so soon Advent will end,
and Christmas Eve is drawing close!

"Spinning is a girl's delight,
through the long sad winter eve;
her work will never come to naught,
this is her firmly bred belief.

"A youth will come to a diligent girl,
he'll say: my girl, come follow me,
be my wife, my love, my world.
I'll be your faithful husband, have me.

"I'll be your husband, you'll be my wife,
give me your hand, my dearest one!

And the girl who spins thread very fine
will sew her wedding gown.

"Spinning wheel, you whir and spin,
soon, so soon Advent will end,
and Christmas Eve is drawing close!"

    II

What good things do you bring us
oh evening, Christmas Eve,
good things to remind us of
your enigmatic feast?

To the farmer, Christmas cake,
cattle have their recompense,
the rooster has his garlic,
the peas are for the hens.

For the fruit trees all the bones
from yesterday's great feasts;
golden piglets on the wall
appear to he who fasts.

Oh, I am a young girl yet,
and my heart is still free:

something's on my mind today,
odd thoughts occur to me.

There on the prince's estate
below, below the woods,
grow the ancient willow trees,
snow on their silver heads.

One humpbacked willow cascades
covertly down like hair,
where the blue lake hides itself
beneath the ice, and there,

it is said, the girls all meet
at midnight; by the moon
they look into the water
to see their future groom.

Midnight doesn't frighten me,
nor does Superstition;
I will go, taking an axe
to cut the ice and look in.

I will look into the lake
into its depths this night.
I'll look upon my future love
steadily, eye to eye.

III

Hana and Marie, two names held dear,
each girl is like a fresh spring rose.
And if you asked anyone who was most dear,
no one could say, for no one knows.

If one of them spoke to a boy, his heart
would burn with fire for her, but then,
moments later he'd completely forget —
with a smile from the second girl!

Now it is midnight, a chorus of stars
is spilling across the wide sky;
they jostle like sheep surrounding a shepherd.
The shepherd's the moon, high, clear, bright.

Midnight has arrived on the night of nights,
midnight of Christmas Eve; on the snow
there are footprints, each fresh and white,
leading to the lake; they're prints we know.

One girl is kneeling over the water;
the second stands next to her:
"Hana, Haničko, my dear golden heart,
what visions do you see there?"

"Oh, I see a cottage, but it's a blur
— now everything is clear —
it's like Václav's cottage — there is a door,
and I see a man standing there!

"He's wearing a jacket — oh, yes, it's dark green —
I know it, I know it! His hat's pulled
low on one side, there's a flower he got from me —
It's Václav himself! Oh dear God!!"

Her heart beating, she rises to her feet;
the second kneels next to her:
"God bless you, what visions do you see?
my golden Marie, my dear!"

"Oh I see, I see — wait, there's a lot of haze,
and red lights flickering through the blur,
everything is obscure with haze,
it seems like the sacristy of a church.

"Something black's floating in a white cloud —
it's becoming clearer — oh, it's
bridesmaids in white, and with them, oh God!
A coffin — and a black crucifix!"

IV

Warm breezes blow and banter
among tender seedlings,
and all the fields and orchards
are blooming charmingly;
sweet music in early morning hours
from the church, an eruption of flowers –
a wedding procession following.

The party surrounds the groom
who's comely as a flower;
he wears a dark green jacket
and a hat pulled lower
on one side: as she saw him that fateful time,
now they're together, he's taking her home,
Hana, his comely bride.

•

Summer's gone; a cold wind blows
across the open fields.
They're taking a body
out on a bier, a bell peals.
Candles blaze, white-clad bridesmaids
are weeping their laments,

a trumpet sounds in the distance,
and *Miserer mei!*

Whose is that green garland,
whose is that sarcophagus?
She's dead, oh, she has died,
the virgin lily! She was fed
as if by dew, and how she flowered.
Then as if cut by a scythe, she withered.
Unfortunate Marie!

V

Winter's here, frost blows at the window;
in the room it's warm by the stove.
An old woman dreams in the fire's glow,
girls spinning linen as she dozes.

"Spinning wheel, you whir and spin,
soon, so soon Advent will end,
and Christmas Eve is drawing close!

"Oh, you Christmas Eve,
a night so wondrously strange!
Every time I think of you,
my heart suffers pangs!

"A year ago we sat
together just as now:
before the year had run its course
we were missing two!

"One, whose head is covered,
is sewing little shirts;
the second, these last three months,
rots in the cold black earth,
unfortunate Marie!

"We sat as we are sitting now,
it seems like yesterday:
and before the year is over
I wonder where we'll be?

"Oh spinning wheel, you whir and spin!
All things on earth have their one turn, then end,
and people's lives are like a dream."

But it's better to be unsure,
to dream and hope in vain,
than to see the awful future
before you, clear and plain!

The Dove

A pretty young widow
walks down the hollowed
cemetery road
weeping with sorrow.

Today she is crying,
accompanying
her husband one last time;
that's why she is grieving.

From a white barnyard
across a green field
rides a handsome young fellow,
feathered hat on his head.

Don't weep, don't cry,
don't ruin those eyes,
pretty young widow,
just heed my advice.

Don't weep, don't moan,
my rose in bloom,
and if your man has died,
take me for your groom.

The first day she cried,
the next, her tears dried,
the third her regret
slowly faded and died.

From that day she ceased
thinking of the deceased:
ere a month had passed
she'd sewn a wedding dress.

The path is so cheery
around the cemetery:
a bride and groom
on their way to marry.

A wedding takes place,
happy and boisterous:
in the arms of her new groom
the bride rejoices.

A wedding takes place,
the music is nice,
the new husband holds his bride
in an embrace. —

Oh laugh and smile, bride,
how well it becomes you:

the wretch six feet under,
his ears can't hear you!

Caress your lover
without any terror:
your husband can't turn over,
the coffin's too narrow.

Kiss them, oh, kiss them,
the cheeks that you crave:
he for whom you mixed the drink
won't come back from the grave.

•

How time flies, time flies,
it's different than before:
what never was will come,
what was will be no more.

How time flies, time flies,
one year is like an hour.
But one thing never dies:
guilt endures forever.

The poor wretch has lain
while three years have passed,

now his burial mound
is covered in green grass.

Yes, green grass is growing,
and there's an oak, still small,
in which a white dove's sitting
above that new green knoll.

It sits and sits and coos,
it coos a grieving song:
and anyone who hears it
is forced to weep along.

It breaks everyone's heart,
especially that woman's
who's tearing at her hair
and crying out in pain:

"Don't murmur in my ears.
Don't coo, don't call:
your cruel, cruel little song
pierces my very soul.

"Don't coo and don't lament,
my head is in a whirl,
or else coo to me then
and break my heart, you bird!" –

Flowing water, flowing,
one wave rolls into the next,
and among the waves
there flits a white dress.

Here we catch a glimpse of leg,
and a white arms waves:
the unhappy woman
is seeking her grave! –

They pull her to the bank,
then dig out on the sly
a grave where the path
crosses into the rye.

She should have been given:
just a large, heavy stone
to weight down her body,
not a grave of her own.

But the curse on her name
weighs more than the stone
that would have been placed
over her dead bones.

Zahor's Bed

I

Silver clouds above the forest heave and glide
like a procession of ghosts, while a crane soars
in flight into a different countryside —
wilderness, fallow fields and orchards.
From the west a cold wind brushes everything;
yellowed leaves softly begin to sing.
Familiar song: every autumn they compose it,
and the oak leaves whisper it anew:
but those who grasp the meaning of the words are few.
It robs the laughter from everyone who knows it.

Unknown pilgrim in the dark habit,
long staff in your hand, with your cross
and your rosary — whoever you are,
whither do you wander beneath the sunset?
With your bare feet in the cold dew
this cold autumn — Where do you hurry so?
We are good people, stay here with us;
everyone is happy to see a good guest. —

But you are still very young, dear pilgrim! —
whiskers don't even cover your chin,

and your cheeks are like those of pretty girls —
except they're pale, so sad, as if touched by frost;
your eyes are sinking in their sockets!
Maybe misfortune, the difficult years
weigh you down, bending your body to earth?
Maybe your heart holds a secret grief.

Don't step into the night, pretty youth!
if we can, we'll be glad to help you.
Only come, lay your body down to rest,
or at least let us bring you some cheer:
there is no sorrow without a cure,
and a powerful balm lies in trust.

He doesn't hear, doesn't know, won't even raise
his eyes. Impossible to coax him from his dreams!
Now he's at the thicket, already on his way:
may God strengthen him on his pilgrimage!

II

An expansive field far, far away;
across the field runs a lengthy lane;
a hill rises to the side of the lane,
and on its peak a slender pine sways
unblemished, even though it's thin.

A tiny hanger's attached to a spike:
it holds a stick on which is pinned
an image of the crucified Christ.
The bloody head bends to the right,
the punctured hands extending wide:
dividing the world between two sides.
The path forks also to each side:
the right, the east, leads to the birth of light;
the left, the west, leads to the night.
In the east are the heavenly gates –
in eternal paradise live God's saints.
To him who does well, He gives hope
so that he will rejoice and exalt.
But in the west are the gates of hell;
a wide sea of pitch enforces them well.
There the demons – cursed band and evil –
weave recalcitrant souls into a flaming wheel.
Let our journey be to the right;
save your children from the left, oh Christ!

There on that hill in the first gleam of dawn,
our young pilgrim on his knees, his fingers wound
around his cross. With tremendous passion
he embraces the unfeeling wood.
Something hisses – tears fall from his eyes –
sighing deep and heavily, again he sighs.

This is the way a young lover departs
just before he leaves his dear maiden,
wending his way into the unknown, he starts
without knowing if they will meet again:
just one more last passionate embrace.
Now be well, oh girl of my desire —
one more ardent, feverish kiss —
unhappy circumstances compel me from here! —

His impenetrable face, an icy visage,
but his heart burns with wild fervor.
Suddenly the pilgrim rises from the earth
and steps toward the western passage. —

Then he disappears in the dense forest thicket:
May God grant His pilgrim some comfort!

III

Deep in the forest there stands a great rock,
next to the path through the ironwood coppice,
and on this great rock, an erect, giant oak,
an ancient king ruling his vast wilderness:
his bare forehead is raised to the sky;
that green spilling over all sides is his shoulders;
his stiff robes are plowed by thunder.

Under his robes his body rots dry:
a spacious hole makes a very pleasant place —
a cozy night's lodging for a fierce forest beast.

And look! On a bed of moss below that oak,
whose is that giant, horrible figure —
a beast or a man in a bearskin cloak?
Few would recognize a man in that creature!
His body — rocks laid one upon another,
his limbs — muscles of oaken logs.
Hair and beard are entangled together,
the face sooty with bushy eyebrows;
and beneath the eyebrows piercing eyes,
venomous eyes, exactly like those
of a snake hidden in green grass.
Who is he? What is he thinking now,
concealed behind his scowling brow?
Who is he? Why does this wilderness draw him? —

Don't ask me anything! Just look, don't ask —
in the coppice on both sides of the path;
ask those bones that lie turning to dust.
Ask these black, unwelcoming guests,
cawing and circling in flight; they see most
everything, and they know even more than they've seen!

Suddenly the woodsman jumps from his bed,
his wild glaring eyes flaring over the road,
waving his enormous club over his head;
with two leaps he's in the middle of the road.

Who is that coming down the path
with a cross in one hand? – The youth in his habit,
and a rosary round his waist! – Run, young man!
Turn back! Your journey leads you to certain death.
Human lives are short enough as it is,
and a virgin youth, it would be such a shame,
turn around, run, while you still have the strength,
before that enormous club falls with a crash
and smashes your little head into bits! –

He doesn't hear, doesn't see, in his deep sorrow,
he goes forth, but his steps are so slow,
to the place where his life must be forfeited. –

"Stand worm!" Who are you? What brings you to this place?"

The pilgrim stops and raises his pale face:
He answers quietly – "I am a reprobate.
I'm on my way to Satan, to hell's own gate!"

"Hoho! To hell? – it's the fortieth year
I've sat here; I have heard much, believe me,

and much have I seen, but this song so far —
no one has yet sung it to me! —
Hoho! To hell? No need to run;
I'll send you there myself, you'll see! —
And when my allotted days are done
I'll follow you there. Don't sigh: there's no need!" —

"Don't blaspheme against God's grace!
Before I saw the light of my first day,
I was inscribed into hell by my father's blood,
by the lies of the devil — for earthly goods.
The sign of the cross — God's grace is great!
It can even break hell's horrible gates,
can defeat Satan in all of his power!
God's grace is great! He deigns to give it,
so that a weak pilgrim returns the victor,
with the contract from hell's dark night." —

"What are you saying? For forty years
I felled, without number, and sent them to hell,
yet no one's returned to tell the tale! —
Listen, worm! You are young, without a beard;
you'd be far tastier than wild, tough beasts,
a delicacy: tonight I would feast.
But I will release you — I'll let you go —
but so far no one, and how many pass through,
have escaped my knotty club until you!

I'll release you, worm! But I want to know:
swear to me you'll relate faithfully
what you learn in hell, and all that you see." —

And the pilgrim raised his staff and rose,
at its tip was the sign of the cross:
"I swear by the cross of the holy saint,
I will bring you news from hell if you wait!"

IV

Winter passed, the snow melts on the mountains,
and floods fill valleys with melted snow, rain;
back from its distant lands comes the crane:
but our pilgrim hasn't come back again.

The sprigs of the forest are dressed in green hues;
the undergrowth exudes the violet's sweet smell;
a nightingale is telling its long tale:
but from the empires of hell there is no news.

Spring passed — summer — the days are growing short;
the leaves are falling, the air has a chill:
there is still nothing from hell to report.
Is the pilgrim coming, do we expect he will?
Has his body fallen on the roadside?
Did hell devour him once he stepped inside? —

The woodsman sits and stares from his high roost
under the oak, scowling into the west.
"How many of them passed," he grumbles,
"and no one has escaped my cudgel!
I've made a deal with one man only,
only this one – and he's betrayed me!"

"O, he hasn't betrayed you!" at that moment
the base cur hears the pilgrim's resonant
voice. The figure erect, the eyes, brave and hard,
cool tranquility across his forehead;
flaming rays emanate as if a sun blazed
behind his pale and noble face.

"God's sinful servant hasn't betrayed you!
I swore an oath, bound myself to you,
and by the cross of the holy saint,
I swear again, I bring you news
from hell – reliable and true!"

Hearing this, the woodsman shakes;
he leaps and reaches for his club:
stunned, as if lightning had struck,
unable to bear the pilgrim's gaze.

"Sit down and hear the horrific tales!
I'll tell you about my walk through hell;

my word gives witness to God's righteous anger:
but God's grace has no end, and it's greater!"

The pilgrim tells what he saw in hell:
ugly devil regiments, sea of flame,
and how, for the damned, death and life are the same:
tortures of hell, always novel, but eternal. —

The woodsman beneath the oak sits frowning,
not saying a word, only glowering.

The pilgrim tells what he heard in hell:
imploring laments — execrable curses —
calling for help — but knowing there is
no one to comfort, no one to help,
just eternal damnation, eternal curses! —

The woodsman beneath the oak sits frowning,
not saying a word, only glowering.

The pilgrim tells how, at the sign of the cross,
Satan, the prince of hell, was forced
to command the devil of the evil lie
to return the bloody contract. The hellish lord
sanctioned the devil who didn't provide
the bloody contract as he was bid.

Satan became enraged and commanded:
"Bathe him in the hellish bath!" – The squad,
according to his instructions,
prepared a fire and ice infusion:
one side burning like flaming coal,
the other side freezing like icy stone;
and when the squad saw the end of his pain,
they turned the frozen one back to the flames.
The devil screamed horribly, writhed like a snake,
until consciousness left him, senses forsaken.
Satan then signaled, the squad stepped aside,
till his strength returned and he revived.
But once he was breathing shallowly,
he clutched the parchment, wouldn't give it away. –

Hopping in anger, Satan commanded:
"Into the infernal iron maiden with him!" –
and the maiden was made of beaten iron,
yearning for mercy, her arms inclined:
she folded the devil to her cruel chest
till all of his bones were crushed.
The devil screamed horribly, writhed like a snake,
until consciousness left him, senses forsaken.
Satan then signaled, the maiden complied
till his strength returned and he revived.
But once he was breathing shallowly,
he clutched the parchment, wouldn't give it away. –

And the final words that Satan said:
"Throw him onto Zahor's bed!"

"To Zahor's bed? To Zahor's bed?" —
His awful body shakes like an aspen,
and sweat breaks out on his forehead,
and the strange woodsman grimly said,
"Zahor's bed! — the name Zahor
was often mentioned by my mother
when she covered me with wolf skin,
when she made my moss bed with rugs.
And now Zahor's bed is in hell, then? —
But answer me — you servant of God,
what awaits Zahor on the hellish bed?" —

"God's vengeance is righteousness, His hand is just,
but His judgments are always hidden.
Although I don't know your hellish anguish,
it doesn't diminish the weight of your sin.
Know that the devil, upon hearing those words,
grew frightened of the tortures of Zahor's
bed, returned the bloody contract as bidden!" —

The centurion fir raises its crown
proudly to the sky, but when an axe
falls, the centurion head bows,
and its fall is so heavy the earth shakes.

The wild forest ox is buoyant with strength;
he uproots the mighty among forest trees:
pierced with a spear, he staggers at length
and falls with a death rattle and wheeze. —

So falls the woodsman, stunned by the news,
shouting and writhing in deathly fright;
beating his head with his fists, on his knees
in the dust, embracing the pilgrim's feet.
"Have mercy, godly man, come to my aid!
don't hand me over to the hellish bed!" —

"Don't speak to me like that! Like you,
I'm a lowly worm; but for God's grace
I'd rot in hell. Ask for help, return to grace,
do penance ere your days are through." —

"What is my penance? See this stick on me,
these rows of notches; it has many —
count them if you can — each mark, each
one, is a murder — every notch!"

The pilgrim lifted Zahor's club from the ground
— the trunk of a great apple tree — and thrust.
It entered the base of the hard rock face
like a thin wand in plowed ground.

"Kneel before the witness of your ghastly crimes,
kneel by day and by night, horrendous villain!
Don't measure thirst and hunger, don't reckon the time,
only reckon your notched row of crime;
repent and plead that God will wipe away
your guilt. Your guilt is great, without precedent:
without precedent must be your penitence,
and God's mercy is limitless!
Kneel and wait – until in time
by the mercy of God I return again."

So speaks the pilgrim and goes on his way. –
And Zahor kneels, kneels continuously;
kneels day and night – doesn't drink, doesn't eat,
groans to God, pleading for mercy –
now snow comes – day after day –
it grows colder; soon there's icy frost,
and Zahor kneels, without break or pause –
but all his waiting is in vain;
the pilgrim doesn't come, return to him.
Let God show mercy to a contrite man!

V

The world keeps spinning, ninety years have flown;
so much has changed in all that time:

those who were babes ninety years ago,
totter to their graves, now very old.
It must be said, those who matured are few;
the rest are all huddled in the grave.
Another generation — faces strange —
wherever there are people, the world is strange:
only the sun and the sky's deep blue,
only those remained without change,
and as they pleased people long ago,
only they can be counted on to please you!

Once more it's spring, and a cool breeze is blowing;
the fresh grass in the meadows is bowing:
once more the nightingale tells his long tale;
once more the new violets exude a sweet smell.

Deep in the woods, in the ironwood's shadow,
two pilgrims are coming down the path:
one has a staff, he's a gnarled old sage,
a bishop's staff, he is shaking with age,
and a pretty young boy at his elbow.

"Wait, my son! I would like to rest,
to be tucked in snugly with our fathers in death;
my soul is requesting some rest!
But the grace of God has chosen else.
God's grace led its servant — it is so great —
powerfully through hell's own gate;

it promoted him to its holy office,
what else can my soul do but bless.
I trusted in your constancy, Lord:
let Your glory settle on the earth! –
My son, I am thirsty! Look around:
I suppose there are no sensual delights
or temptations, but there is water nearby,
so that my life's work will come to an end."

The young man leaves to go exploring
through the woods for the hidden spring;
he struggles through the coppice, crawling on
until he exits at a mossy stone.
But suddenly his footsteps cease;
his pretty cheek shines with wonder
as if lit by an evening fire:
an exotic fragrance arrives on a breeze,
indescribable fragrance, unending charm,
as if he had entered an Edenic orchard.
And once the youth has cleared the scrub,
he reaches for the rock and climbs up;
he sees something indescribable:
a great tree stands on the bare rock face;
its spread is immense. It is an apple,
fruit ripens on it with beauty and grace –
golden apples – and a heavenly smell
clings to them, surrounds the forest as well.

And the heart rejoices inside the boy,
and his lively eyes sparkle with joy:
"Oh, surely, surely! our good God's hand
is working a miracle for the old man:
– instead of water, fresh and cold –
heavenly fruits that grow from a stone."

He reaches for an apple, but when he nears,
he suddenly withdraws his hand in fear.

"Stop, don't pluck – if you didn't plant!"
a hollow voice stiffly commands,
a voice so close as if from the ground,
but he sees nobody else around;
a big stump is the only thing close,
blackberries wind around its moss,
not far the remains of an ancient oak,
a shattered trunk with a wide hollow.

He peers in the hollow, circles the stump,
examines the woods, each bulge and lump:
but he can't find anything that would show
anyone ever set foot there before,
just empty wilderness, nothing more.

"Maybe my ears are playing tricks?
some wild animal roared in the distance?

Maybe it's the sound of a spring in the rock?"
he says to himself, the pretty young boy,
and reaches for the apple, ignoring the voice.

"Stop, don't pluck — if you didn't plant!"
a hollow voice, this time with more force.
When the young man looks around for the voice,
the stump between the blackberries begins
to move; from the moss two long arms extend,
reach for the boy, and smoldering like pitch,
above the arms, like candles in the mist,
two black eyes from beneath the gray moss
turn on him and study his face.

The young man cowers, makes the sign of the cross,
signs once, signs twice, three times he signs,
and like a frightened merlin out of its nest,
not seeking the path or noting obstacles,
he flies from the rock, through the thicket, blind,
bloody from thorns and sharp, spiky vines;
he falls to the earth near the old man.

"Oh, sir, sir! There is evil in this wood:
on a rocky plain, a spreading apple tree;
the apples are ripe, although it's just spring;
so no one can pluck them a big stump stands guard.
And that stump speaks, and he can see,

his arms catch whoever approaches the tree:
oh, sir, the devil is reigning!"

"My son, you are wrong! Here God's grace
is at work — glory be to Him!
I see that my journey is at its end.
My body will gladly take its place
in the earth! — Serve me one last time, my son!
lead me up to the rocky plain."

The young man did so, cleared the path to the plain,
then returned to carry the old man again. —

And when they come up to the apple tree,
oh! the stump inclines to the old man, reaching
out his arms to him and rejoicing: "Oh sir,
my lord, for so long you didn't return.
Look, your sapling is bearing fruit!
Oh, pluck, sir! For you yourself planted it!"

"Zahor! Zahor! May peace be with you:
In my last days, peace I bring you!
God's grace is without measure, without end,
it pulled us both from the hellish bed!
Release me now, as I release you, even
let our ashes die down side by side,
let the angels take our spirits to heaven!"

And the instant Zahor said "Amen!"
he shivered into a humble mound
of ash. The blackberry vines on the bare stone,
all the memory of him that remained.

Just then the old man dropped dead to the earth —
his pilgrim tasks completed in this world! —
And the young man remained alone in the forest
to fulfill the will of his lord.

But in that instant, high above him,
two white doves are hovering;
they hover rejoicing then disappear
up into the angelic sphere.

Water Sprite

I

Over the lake in a poplar tree
sat a sprite one evening:
"Shine sweet moonlight shine,
I stitch a dainty line.

"I sew, I sew me little boots
to wear in wet and dry pursuits:
Shine sweet moonlight shine,
I stitch a dainty line.

"Today is Thursday, Friday's next,
I sew a jacket with a vest:
Shine sweet moonlight shine,
I stitch a dainty line.

"Green suit, with boots of cherry,
tomorrow I will marry:
Shine sweet moonlight shine,
I stitch a dainty line."

II

At dawn the young girl rose,
made a bundle of her clothes.
"At the lake, my mother, sweet,
I'll make my clothing clean and neat."

"Oh no, sweet child, not to the water!
Stay home today, my little daughter!
A strange dream came to me last night.
Oh, stay inside and out of sight:

"I chose pearls for you last night
and dressed you in a gown of white
made of froth and foam, my dear.
Don't go outside! Stay with me here!

"White cloaks sadness – heed my fears –
and pearls are soft and round as tears,
and Friday's an unlucky day.
Don't go outside, my daughter, stay!"

She's so restless, restless daughter,
something draws her to the water,
to the water. Nothing she knows,
nothing she longs for. Still, she goes.

As her first cloth touches the lake
the bridge beneath her starts to break.
Down she goes, just like a pearl,
and water closes over the girl.

From below, the waves roll in,
a ring is spreading wide and thin.
Beside the rocks a poplar stands,
on it a green man claps his hands.

III

Cheerless and dismal
the watery lands
where fishes play together
beneath water lily stands.

Sunshine doesn't reach there,
breezes never blow –
cold, silent as grief
in a heart that's lost all hope.

Cheerless and dismal
the watery world,
as twilight turns to dusk
a new day is unfurled.

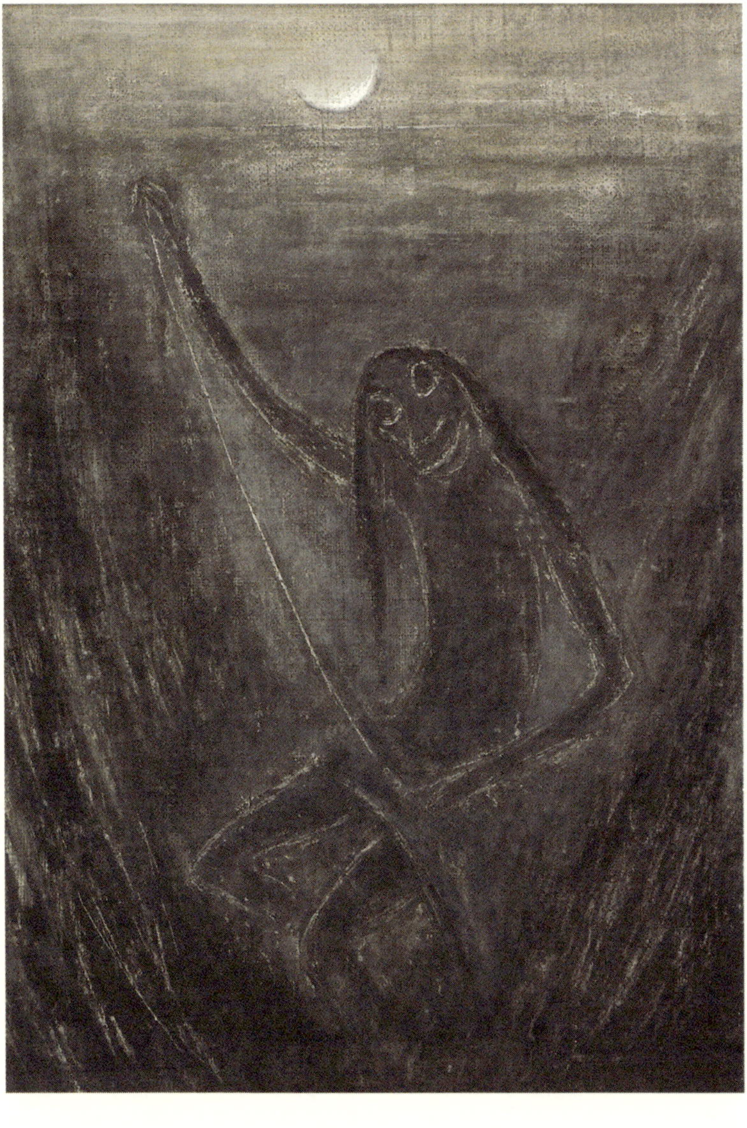

Water Sprite's yard is spacious,
wealth and plenty in it.
But almost no one passes by,
no one dares to visit.

Whoever enters once
through his crystal door
is never ever seen again —
nor heard from anymore.

Water Sprite sits at the door,
mends carefully his nets,
and his soft young wife
holds a baby to her breast.

"Rock-a-bye my baby,
the child I did not seek.
You are smiling at me,
but I am dead with grief.

"You open joyful arms to me,
you wrap your arms around.
But right now I would rather lie
in a grave there on dry ground.

"In the earth behind the church
next to a black cross,

so that my golden mother
would be very close.

"Rock-a-bye, my little son,
my little water sprite.
How could I not think of Mother
when my tears fall day and night?

"Poor mother planned to find me
a handsome young groom.
But before it all could happen
I was stolen from my home.

"So now I'm married, married now —
but there was some mistake:
The groomsmen — black crawdads,
and the bridesmaids — pike!

"And my husband! — God have mercy!
His feet are wet on dry land.
And in the lake, beneath teacups,
he collects the souls of humans.

"Rock-a-bye, my little son,
my little green-haired boy.
Your mother didn't marry
into a house of joy.

"Deceived and caught
in nets of guile,
she has no joy
but you, my child."

"What are you singing, my wife?
Give me some relief!
Your damned singing hurts my ears
and angers me beyond belief!

"Don't sing anything, my wife!
It makes my heart pound in my chest!
Don't make me change you to a fish
as I've done to all the rest."

"Don't be angry, don't be angry,
my husband, Water Sprite!
Don't be angry with a rose
that once was fresh and bright.

"You tore the flower
of my happy youth in two.
Then you never did a thing
to make me think kindly of you.

"I've begged a hundred times,
let sweet words intercede,

let me see my mother,
a short time's all I need.

"I've begged a hundred times —
each day I plead and cry —
to see my mother just once more,
bid her a last goodbye.

"I've begged a hundred times
upon my poor bent knees.
Your crusty heart won't soften,
and you never try to please.

"Don't be angry, don't be angry,
Water Sprite, my lord,
or else — fine then, be angry,
and keep your awful word!

"And if you want me as a fish —
blind and deaf and still,
you'd better turn me to stone
without memory or will.

"You'd better turn me to stone —
thoughtless, senseless — and be done —
so I won't mourn eternally
that I can't see the sun."

"I'd like to trust your word, my wife,
but a fish in the wide, wide sea . . .
How could I catch her again
and bring her home to me?

"I'd not prevent your seeing
your mother for a day.
But I'm terribly afraid
of a cunning woman's way.

"Thus I will allow you
to leave me for a day,
but listen to what I command
and promise to obey.

"Don't embrace your mother,
any human under the sun.
Otherwise your love on land
will kill your watery one.

"Don't embrace a single soul
from dawn until day's end,
and before night falls again,
come back to me beneath the lake.

"From dawn to dusk I'm giving you
to be away from me.

But you must leave the baby here
as a guarantee."

IV

What's an Indian summer
without sun on your face?
What's a joyful reunion
without a teary embrace?
After what seemed like forever
the daughter flew to her mother.
Who'd fault the daughter for that hug,
call her broken word disgrace?

The lake lady and her mother
cried all day for joy. "Dear
golden mother, goodbye!
Evening's coming, how I fear!"
"Don't worry, my dear soul,
don't fear that murdering ghoul!
I won't allow you to be —
in the water monster's power!"

Evening comes — A green man
walks across the yard.
A latch — the door is fastened,

the girl's inside, mother's on guard.
"My dear soul, don't worry,
he can't harm you where it's dry,
here on dry land above,
the lake-murderer's power is barred."

As soon as the bells toll evening,
Knock! Knock! outside the door.
"Come home! Come home, my wife!
I haven't had my supper!"
"Go away, leave our door,
you scheming murderer!
And what you once ate in the lake,
Go eat it as before!"

At midnight, Knock! Knock! once again
upon the weathered door.
"Come home! Come home, my wife,
come make my bed once more!"
"Go away, leave our door,
you scheming murderer!
And whoever used to make your bed
let them make it as before!"

And for the third time, Knock! Knock!
at the rising of the sun.
"Come home! Come home, my wife!

Come nurse our weeping son!"
"Oh, Mother, I'm wild, wild!
My heart is breaking for my child!
Oh, Mother, golden mother, sun!
Let me go, I have to run!"

"The water murderer will betray.
Don't go anywhere, my dear.
Even if you fear for your baby,
so much greater is my fear.
Away to the water, murderer,
my daughter shan't go anywhere!
And if your baby is hungry,
bring it to our door."

A baby cries through the storm
that rages on the lake.
The cry pierces the soul
and then the cry goes slack.
"Oh, my mother, oh my God!
That cry is curdling my blood!
Oh my golden mother,
I'm terrified of the water sprite!"

Something fell — under the door
a liquid flooded — bloody red.
The mother opens cautiously
trembling in dread.

Two things lay there in the blood —
fear froze her where she stood —
a baby's body with no head,
a head without its body.

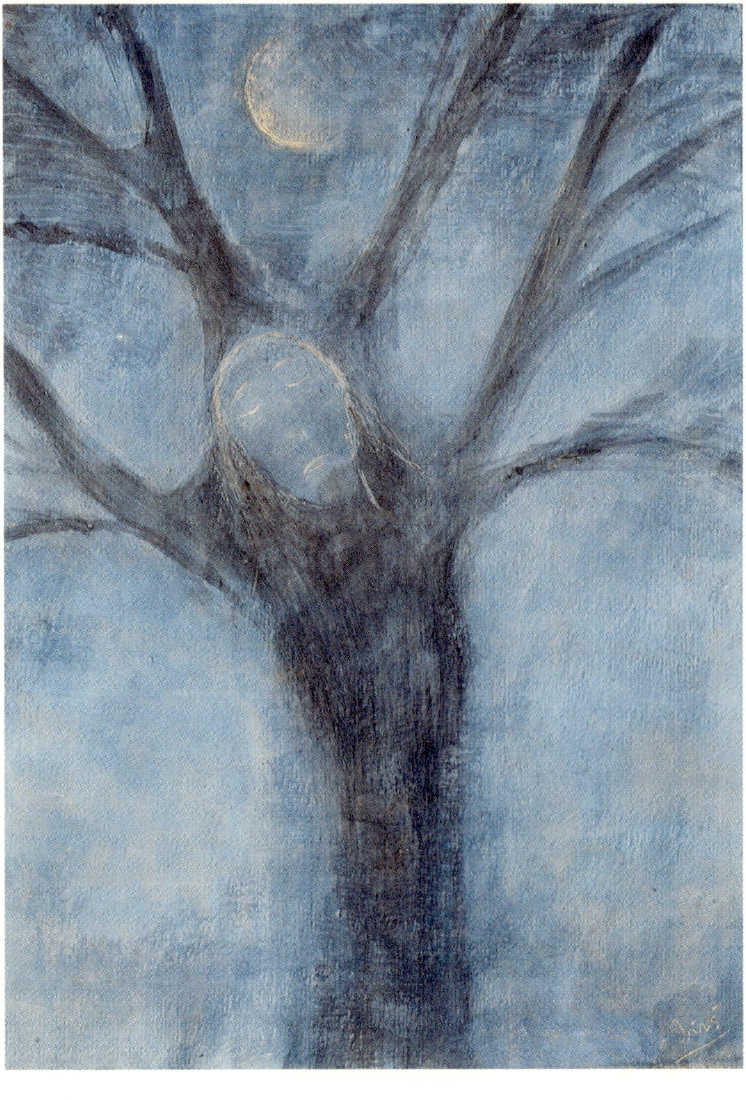

Willow

Breakfasting, grease on his knife,
a man beseeches his young wife,

"When I've questioned you, my wife,
you've answered me, my dear, my life,

"always answered me, my wife,
except just once, my dear, my life.

"We're together now two years,
and only one thing stirs my fears.

"My dear wife, my light,
what happens when you sleep each night?

"Each evening, sound, you go to bed,
but in the night it's like you're dead.

"Not a movement, not a prayer,
and your spirit isn't there.

"Your body's cold and still as lead.
It really seems as if you're dead.

"Even when our baby screams
it doesn't shake you from your dreams.

"My lovely, precious wife,
does illness threaten your life?

"If it's illness, let us see,
maybe there's a remedy.

"Maybe fragrant herbs that grow
in the fields can make you whole.

"And if there is no healing plant,
perhaps we'll find a magic chant.

"A word can change the sky,
keep storm-struck sailors safe and dry.

"A magic word can order fire,
break rocks, harness a dragon's ire,

"tear bright stars from the skies at night.
A mighty word will make you right."

"Oh, my husband, my dear lord,
won't you heed my honest word.

"For what's given as destiny
there isn't any remedy.

"What the Fates ordain for you
a human word cannot undo.

"Though nights, my spirit leaves my bed,
the power of God rests on my head.

"God's strength protects me every night,
as day is held in streams of light.

"Though I sleep as if I'm dead,
mornings my soul returns to bed.

"And in the morning I can stand,
healthy, fresh, through God's command." –

Lady, speeches are in vain,
your husband's got another plan.

A fire is burning on the knoll,
a crone pours water from bowl to bowl,

twelve bowls of water, still as ice.
The husband asks the crone's advice.

"Look, Mother, you know everything,
even what the future brings.

"You know whence an illness grows,
you know where the Death Woman goes.

"Tell me clearly, do not hide.
What is happening to my bride?

"Each evening, sound, she goes to bed,
but in the night it's like she's dead.

"Not a movement, not a prayer,
and her spirit isn't there.

"Her body's cold and still as lead.
It really seems as if she's dead." —

"Is it odd she's dead when your wife
has only half: her daylight life?

"By day she's with the child, she's yours,
but nights her soul sleeps in osiers.

"Go to the stream below the park,
you'll find a willow with white bark.

"Its osiers form a golden bowl,
and there each night resides her *soul*."

"I want a wife who sleeps with me,
not one who lives in a willow tree!

"May my wife be bound to me,
and let it rot, that willow tree!"

He cut the willow at the root,
then leaned his axe against his boot.

The willow heaved into the stream,
and as it fell, there was a scream.

Then it moaned and then it sighed,
sad, as if a mother died.

A dying mother, it turned back to clasp
her child before her last collapse.

"Why are they rushing to my door?
A tolling bell, I wonder what for?"

"Your dear young wife died today
in the quickest, strangest way.

"At her chores, as sound as can be,
then she fell, just like a tree.

"With her dying breath she sighed
looking back to see her child."

"Oh, woe is me! Oh, woe, oh woe!
I killed my wife! I didn't know!

"And this baby that we had —
I have an orphan, small and sad.

"Oh willow, white willow! Oh, willow tree,
why have you tormented me?

"You've taken half my life with you,
tell me now, what should I do?"

"Remove me from my watery tears,
cut off my golden osiers.

"Have me cut into boards, and then
make a cradle out of them.

"On my breast let the little one lie,
and may the poor thing never cry.

"And with the cradle's to and fro,
his mother holds him, soft and slow.

"Spread the osiers along the stream
to keep harm far away from him.

"When he grows older, give him a knife,
and he'll have whistles all his life.

"And every time he pipes he'll hear
his mother speaking to her dear."

Lily

Dies a young maid in the spring of her years,
as when a rosebud suddenly dries;
rose in the bud, a maiden dies –
lies in the earth, what a shame she must lie!

"Don't lay me down in the village graveyard,
where laments of orphans and widows are heard,
tears without measure that bring no relief,
there would my heart pine away in grief.

"Bury me in the green forest instead,
heather will bloom there around my head;
birds will sing for me day and night,
there will my heart rejoice and delight."

Ere a year and a day had passed,
a small cover of heather amassed;
before the third year had expired,
the heather on her grave had flowered.

White lily – whoever lays eyes upon her
feels a strange pang in his heart start to stir;
fragrant lily – who breathes her scent,
the fire of longing will be sweet torment.

"Hey, my servants, bring me my horse!
I want to hunt beneath the green forest,
I want to hunt beneath fir trusses:
I have a strange feeling today's hunt is precious!"

Halloho! Hallo! the barking of greyhounds.
Ditch or no ditch — hops! — fence or no fence: bounds
the lord on his horse with his weapon inclined,
like the arrow before him flies a white hind.

"Halloho! Hallo! my precious deer,
neither field nor brush will grant you succor!"
His arm raised to shoot, the arrow ready,
but instead of a hind — a white lily.

The lord regards the lily, amazed;
his arm falls, his breath is bated;
he thinks and thinks, his breast rises —
who understands? — with fragrance or desire?

"Get to work, my faithful servants,
careful now, dig up the lily; I want
her in my garden — I don't know why,
it seems that without her I will die!

"Hey, my faithful servants, hey my friends,
guard the lily and carefully tend,

carefully tend it night and day —
strange its power, I'm under its sway!"

He tends it the first day and then the next;
her presence makes him feel oddly blessed.
But the third night, full moon in the skies,
swiftly the servant: "My lord, arise,

something's wrong, a mistake. My lord,
your lily moves through the orchard,
hurry, don't stall, get up and get changed,
your lily is speaking, her voice is so strange!" —

"My life is ephemeral, sadly concealed,
like steam on the river, like dew in the field,
my transient life: with the dawning of the day,
the dew, the steam, and my life fade away."

"Your time won't end, I have faith, I believe;
four solid walls will give you relief.
I will build you shelter from the sun:
just be my wife, my soul, my one."

She married him and they lived in bliss;
she even gave birth to a son. The lord, his
joy complete, gave a banquet, but before the toast
his royal livery brings him a post.

"My dear faithful lord!" the king writes,
"be ready tomorrow to serve me, to fight;
I require each faithful lord to come,
the need is great — leave everything at home."

He bid his dear wife a sad adieu
saying, "I cannot be here to guard you;
I charge my mother with your protection."
But his heart was heavy with premonition.

Poorly his mother fulfilled his will,
she did not protect his wife very well:
demolished chamber, sun high in the sky —
"Die, night lady, die monster, die!"

His duty discharged, he turns home, making haste,
but grievous news meets him on the way:
"Your baby is no longer alive —
your lily has faded, that is, your dear wife!"

"Mother, what did you have against my wife?
You poisoned the flower of my life:
O Mother, you are an evil snake,
may your life in God's world be black!"

A Daughter's Curse

Why are you so somber,
      my daughter?
Why are you so somber?
How glad you always were!
    Where did your laughter go?

I killed a little dove,
      my mother!
I killed a little dove –
forlorn as an unmatched glove –
    it was white, as white as snow.

It was no little dove,
      my daughter!
it was no little dove –
Your face is so ravaged,
    you seem altered beyond belief!

Ach, I killed my baby
      my mother!
ach, I killed my baby,
pathetic newborn baby –
    I think I'll die right now of grief!

How will you atone,
      my daughter?
how will you atone?
atone for what you've done,
      stave off the wrath of God?

I'll go and seek that bloom,
      my mother!
I'll go and seek that bloom
that takes away all blame
      and cools the stormy blood.

And where will you find this flower,
      my daughter?
and where you will find this flower,
in all the wide world over?
      in which garden does it grow?

Behind the gate on the hill,
      my mother!
behind the gate on the hill
on the post with a nail
      it blooms on a noose made of rope!

What words will you leave the boy,
      my daughter?

what words will you leave the boy
who used to come and enjoy
   our home and your company?

This is his blessing from me,
      my mother!
This is his blessing from me —
a worm in his soul for eternity
   for lying so treacherously!

And what will you leave your mother,
      my daughter?
and what will you leave your mother,
who loved you more tenderly than any other,
   who doted on you each day?

I leave you a curse
      my mother!
I leave you a curse
that even in death you'll find no rest,
   for you always let me have my way!

The Prophetess

Fragments

When your eyes well up with tears,
my hope will branch out like a tree;
when you fall on difficult years,
my voice will sound my prophesy.

Stop weighing my words lightly, listen:
the spirit of prophecy comes from heaven.
Everyone pays his due in the end –
the principle on which the world stands.

The river seeks its end in the sea,
a flame finds its peak in the sky.
It will return, what the earth creates,
but nothing is vain, nothing is futile.

Fate's course is fixed, her steps are firm,
what has to happen will happen.
What's buried one day in the flow of time
will resurface at that day's end.

•

I saw a man on Bělina Voda –
the forefather of our famous dukes
at his plow behind the village steps,
cultivating the land for crops.

Messengers from the plenary assembly
said the plowman was invited by the prince;
they dressed him in gold, attired him finely,
but the field is barren and the plowing unfinished.

"Go back to where you came from!" he said,
releasing the oxen, he put down the plow;
he dug his stick into the field,
that it would sprout leaves and flowers.

A nearby mountain swallowed the oxen;
to this day it carries a wet, slimy mark –
and three fertile hazelnut sprigs
sprout from a dry strip of bark.

All three twigs bloomed and brought forth fruit,
but two fell and withered away.
Only one of the three bore mature fruit,
the other two haven't grown since that day.

Hear and know – let my voice not be in vain!
Place it firmly in your memory, accept it:

there will come a time, there will come a day
when even dead blight will be resurrected.

Both withered branches of the noble flower
will increase, gather width and girth;
they will bear, in an unexpected hour,
good fruit, to the amazement of the world.

There will come a prince who will pay an old debt,
dressed in gold and purple,
and he will restore Přemysl's plow, abject
as it is from its filth and dust, to the world.

And he will call up the oxen from the hollow
mountain, he'll return to the neglected field,
he'll harness the oxen to the plow
and will sow golden grains for a golden yield.

And the seedlings will emerge and will blossom
in the spring, and in summer will yield golden ears:
then to the land will happiness come,
and the ancient glory will reappear.

•

I saw Krok's castle in gold
on a rock towering over the river;

surrounding the castle a blooming field,
Princess Libuše's orchard in flower.

Down below the castle, a dear little house —
the princess's bath on the river;
I saw the princess's noble face
above glowing robes of silver.

On the threshold of her bath she gazed
at the muddy river current;
there she read words that encouraged and amazed:
her dear land's secret judgment.

"I see fires and bloody wars,
I see your misery, your denigration;
you will be pierced by a bloody sword,
but don't despair, my nation!"

Now two maidens standing close
hand her a cradle of gold;
she kisses it, drops it to the rock's base
beneath the river's unfathomable flow.

Hear and know Libuše's utterance —
I heard her voice's prophecy:
"Stay here, dear cradle of my son
until I call you back to me!

"A young, new world will arise, strong and hard
from the dark womb of the sea;
the broad lindens in my father's backyard
will bloom again, fragrant, abundant and sweet.

"Torrential rain will vivify the sad green corn;
the night will yield to a clear, new day:
this nation will soon be reborn,
glorious as it was in its former fame.

"The golden cradle, with its child resting there,
will emerge from the river's abyss:
the salvation of our land is secure
when this age-old judgment comes to pass."

•

I saw you, couch of paradise!
I know you already, my star, know you're mine!
But when will I see you with my own eyes? —
this question puzzles my peaceful mind.

Summer after summer, without end,
and winter rushes past winter:
my faith still stands unshaken,
hope grows from year to year.

In summer many bodies will not come back
from the waters beneath the rock. When it's cold,
the weight of sleighs causes ice to crack.
I am sighing with sorrow: behold!

Libuše's regiment has increased,
has added new members once more!
When is it time for my labor to cease?
When the prophecy's fulfilled, not before!

Hear and know my warning.
It is written in books, it's destiny:
"In the dawn of that joyful morning,
death will stand in its glory.

"Then Libuše, with her great regiment,
will gather her watery troops at their station,
and her motherly hand will lift them;
she'll bring fame to her own Czech nation!"

•

Above the river Orlice I saw a church
and heard its golden bell. It extinguished
the rush of fierce passions first,
then the ancient Czech sincerity.

When Czech's godly virtues — love, hope, and faith —
turned musty and stale from disuse,
the church hid itself in the depths of the earth,
and water then flooded the place.

But it will not always remain drowned;
the water will flow away again;
the glorious voice of the bell will sound,
and the church will rise up in its former acclaim.

Hear and know, so it is written,
so it is set in the wheel of fortune:
"When the golden bell awakens
there will dawn a glorious golden morn.

"The wind will sow a new wood
on yon side of the Orlice River;
after the young trees grow and grow old,
this pine will finally mature.

"And when, at the edge of the forest,
this pine reaches its final day,
it will wither and fall into the Orlice,
and even its roots will decay.

"At that time a wild swine will root out and tear
the last remnants of the gutter,

and the golden bell will reappear
from the ruined debris and the clutter.

"From the beginning it was ordained
the bell would travel underground
until reaching its goal: it would remain
beneath the river and wait to sound."

Know this: on the slope below the green pines,
tall and strong, with very few limbs,
the predestined tree already ripens,
its fresh top swaying on its stem.

Is the bell already underway?
Will it reach in time its destination?
Who will tell us, who can say,
who will strengthen the faith of our nation?

I saw a peasant at his plow,
in the field near Bystřice,
humbly singing his morning song:
"O God, Holy Trinity!"

A strange obstruction hit the plow,
knocked the blade from its furrow, as if with a tap:
"What devil in hell froze it up so?
May he fall into his own damned trap!"

So the plowman cursed and his shrill voice fell
into the hole that stymied him –
in response, the lamenting cry of the bell:
"It's not yet time, oh it's not yet time!"

It's not yet time, oh it's not yet time!
if you lay your ear to the ground
at the root of the fir, that distant chime
is the golden bell's sorrowful sound.

•

Don't lament unhappiness, the fate
that seems so difficult in your eyes.
You should lament instead that
it hasn't yet made you wise!

Aye! I see one mountain higher than another –
the mountain you know well –
lush orchards all around her,
and on that mountain a cathedral.

Three gates lead into the cathedral, and three
gates lead out again as well;
hear and know, place this voice of prophecy
in your heart, for this writing will be fulfilled:

"You cherish this wishful thinking in vain!
Despair and poverty will be your lot
until the tough Czech people, in time,
will enter through *only one* gate!"

Who has ears, then let him hear,
why plug them with your fingers? And if
heaven's own wisdom has come to you here,
why let it fall beneath your feet?

Svatopluk taught his sons to cooperate
already a thousand years ago.
But his wise words didn't penetrate
your understanding until now!

•

You who know of the glorious deeds
of your fathers, you like to boast of them:
on a pillar in Prague you will see
half a hero standing by the bridge.

The head weathered, washed down by rain;
the Swedish war broke the chest,
but the belly and legs still stand,
as well as the foolish proud dress.

Don't speak in vain: "You feeble old stones
of ancient ages, of yesterday!"
Know that this is a fateful sign
for your heroes of today!

Listen well and weigh my word:
Don't boast with hope, save that
above the stomach a new hot heart
and a genuine head will sprout!

Author's Notes

A BOUQUET

This legend on the origins of thyme (or similar herb) comes from the former Klatovy Region of Bohemia, and it is undoubtedly based on an interpretation of the very word itself in Czech – *mateřídouška*, a compound of "mother" and "breath" [alt. "soul"]. In Polish, the herb is similarly called *macierzaduszka* or *macierzanka*, and the South Slavic has something akin to this as well. In Old Church Slavonic it is simply called *dushitsa*, which is also how it is used in Russian.

THE TREASURE

This legend is known throughout Europe, variously altered only in the particulars. In old Czech literature we find it woven into the legend of St. Clement, the Pope, whom the Roman Emperor Trajan had drowned in the sea having ordered an anchor tied around his neck. Legend has it that each year on the day of his demise, and for seven days thereafter, the sea would part for three miles so that pilgrims could walk on dry land to where a marble shrine stood, miraculously created to house the body of St. Clement in a magnificent sarcophagus. It is told that once a woman came with her child through the parted sea on the seventh day, and when the child fell asleep, the sea suddenly began to roar and close up again. Overcome by fear, the woman forgot her child and ran for the shore with the others; once there, she remembered the child. Lamenting and crying, she searched at length if the sea had cast her dead child onto the shore, and returning home distraught, she spent the entire year immersed in sorrow. When a year had passed and the sea once again parted, she rushed ahead of everyone else to be the first at St. Clement's tomb, and looking around she saw that, yes, her child was there in the same place where she had left him, sleeping. Waking the child and, overjoyed, cradling him in her arms, she asked him where he had been this whole year? The child replied: "Have I slept a year or only a single night."

The Passion is sung in the choir.

Folklore has it that during Holy Week as the Passion is being sung all earthly treasures open up, thus the basis for this legend.

WEDDING SHIRTS
In Bohemia, this legend is told in two essentially different versions, though it is true that both are remnants of folk songs common to the region. In one version a corpse beseeches a young maiden to come with him with these words:

> Rise my love! Rise and lace up,
> my time is short, no time to delay;
> my horse is swift as gunshot,
> we'll cover 100 miles by break of day.

Folk songs and tales that tell of a corpse rising from the grave to go to the girl he loved while alive, or the beloved might be a sister, are found in nearly all Slavic cultures and among other nations. The Serbs have a song about dead Yovan who comes on a sepulchral horse to his sister, Yelitza. Slovaks tell it with the girl summoning her dead lover, cooking the dead man's head in boiling porridge, its voice calling through the steam: "Come, come, come!" In Little Russia [Ukraine] they have a folk song similar to that of the Serbs. The Russian version of the legend is dressed up in a poem by Zhukovsky, just as the Polish, or Lithuanian, is by Mickiewicz. The German ballad *Lenore* by Gottfried Bürger is generally well known. A Scottish folk song has sweet William's ghost visiting his fair Margaret, while an old Breton song tells of a brother who, having fallen in battle, comes at night to take off his poor beloved sister, named Gwennolaik, to the other world. This remarkable currency of one and the same myth among peoples distant in geography and language clearly points to its ancient origins. Related to it are the legends of vampires and werewolves, which are as prevalent among the Slavs as they are among many other European nations.

And your body, lovely, white,
would have ended like these shirts.

That is, torn into pieces. In Slavic myth, a young girl leaves her furs with a vampire as suchlike ruse to get free of him. When midnight comes, the vampire first devours the furs and then goes for the girl, who is hiding in her home. The vampire beats on the door, while the girl uses various pretexts to keep him at bay outside until the cock crows.

NOON WITCH

As at midnight, noon, too, according to folklore, has its maleficent beings, and the hour between eleven and twelve is when they exercise their ruinous power. This type is called a "noon witch" or generally a "wild woman." Venturing into the woods at noontime is therefore shunned lest a wild woman fogs one's mind.

THE GOLDEN SPINNING WHEEL
This legend is found in the first volume of Božena Němcová's collection.* Moreover, a similar version exists among the folktales of Southern Russia.

"Fetch me living water, my boy"

Living water actually means water in summer, running water; so dead water is that of winter, frozen. Slavic folklore attributes such power to living water that any sort of body, even one putrid with decay, will be reanimated once immersed in it. If someone should pour it into the sea, the sea would burst into flames. In Russian legends, the difference between living and dead water is that the latter is able to make a body that has been cut into pieces whole while the former gives this reunited body life. The implication is that water generally has the power to give strength and rejuvenate.

Whirrr – evil is the thread you spin!

Just as the whirring of the spinning wheel here reveals that a murder has been committed, in other common folktales of Czechs, Poles, and Ukrainians the same is performed by a willow whistle.

---

* Erben is referring here to *Národní báchorky a pověsti* (Folk Tales and Legends), the first volume of which was published in 1845.

CHRISTMAS EVE

For Slavs, no other day is accompanied by such a general practice of divination as Christmas Eve. The farmer, the wife, the young lad, the maiden all try to discover and predict what the following year holds for them. The methods of such fortunetelling are rather diverse, and it is virtually impossible to enumerate them all. Described here is one that is very common to Bohemia for a young girl who wishes to learn which man is destined for her.

To the farmer, Christmas cake,
cattle have their recompense,

A Christmas cake or a bread roll is given to a farmer as a wish that he have abundant crops the coming year and, especially, that his fields be full of wheat. The evening's leftovers are fed to the cows that they should give plenty of milk. The lady of the house gives the rooster a strip of garlic for high spirits and throws a handful of peas to the hens that they lay many eggs. The leftover fishbones are buried under fruit trees to boost their yield in the coming year. And since a strict fast is observed all day till evening, it is promised to children who keep the fast that at night they will see a golden piglet.

THE DOVE

He for whom you mixed the drink
won't come back from the grave.

To mix something for someone implies poison and is generally used instead of the verb "to poison."

and there's an oak, still small,
in which a white dove's sitting

In Slavic folktales and songs the soul of a person who has died without any guilt or has been cleansed of guilt most often appears as a white dove, and the dove as stand-in for the soul takes on a darker hue commensurate with the degree of guilt found in the deceased, or even takes the form of another type of bird until ultimately the criminal soul metamorphoses into a raven.

ZAHOR'S BED
This legend is known in Bohemia, Poland, and Lusatia. The Czech name Záhoř becomes Madej in Polish folktales and Lipskulijan in Sorbian. The content and story line of this tale have their origins in early Christianity.

"Into the infernal iron maiden with him!"

The Czech chroniclers give accounts of a certain instrument of death known as an iron maiden, employed for noblemen sentenced to death for their crimes yet whom the courts did not want to deliver into the hands of the executioner. One such iron maiden stood in a chamber of the White Tower in Prague.

But in that instant, high above him,
two white doves are hovering;

See the previous note to "The Dove."

WATER SPRITE

It is worth remembering that all mythical creatures of water found in the legends of Slavs and other nations usually harbor a distinct cruel streak, and when such a creature could not take revenge on a human it would turn on its own kind. It should also be noted that an analogous tale is also told of a "Woodwose," a wild man of the woods, who snatches a young girl and for seven years keeps her as his wife. And when she runs away, he takes his revenge by tearing into pieces the children he has fathered with her. A similar legend of the water sprite is found in a Sorbian folk song.

Shine sweet moonlight shine,
I stitch a dainty line.

In our versions of the tale, the water sprite sings this to himself while sitting at night in a poplar by the water, sewing his boots.

His feet are wet on dry land.

It is said that one of the ways a water sprite can be recognized among people is by the fact that the left side of his clothes is always dripping water.

And in the lake, beneath teacups,
he collects the souls of humans.

Bubbles that sometimes rise from the depths of a pond or lake to the surface, as if someone underneath had tipped over a vessel covering him and allowed the air in it to escape, gave rise to the legend that a water sprite keeps the souls of drowned persons trapped under little pots below.

My little green-haired boy

A water sprite and his offspring have, according to legend, green hair.

Don't embrace your mother,
any human under the sun.

Unique to the Bohemian versions of the tale is that whenever anyone from another world of any kind returns to this one, the warning is oft-repeated that they should embrace and kiss no one lest they forget everything that came before and thus lose what is most dear to them.

WILLOW
Compared to the others, this tale seems important to me because no analogy is found among other Slavs or any other nation. To be sure, there are myths where a person metamorphoses into a tree or into some other thing, and vice versa; and there are myths as well where the soul leaves the human body at night in the form of a mouse, bird, or snake, the body lying lifeless until its animal incarnation returns to it. But as far as I am aware, this is the sole example of a folktale where the human form and something other – here a tree – share life, whereby neither the human being nor the thing can exist without the other for long. The legend comes from the former Bydžov Region of Bohemia.

A mighty word will make you right.

A mighty word is understood as an incantation or a magic spell (*incantatio, Zauberspruch*), to which great importance is attached in mythology.

*What the Fates ordain for you
a human word cannot undo.*

It is said that when a child is born the three Fates visit him at night to determine what his future will be. One says: "His destiny is this." The second says: "No, his destiny will be this." And it is always left to the third to decide the matter. Croats call them the *Rojenice*.

A crone pours water from bowl to bowl,

Divination from water is a practice common to all Slavic peoples.

You know where the Death Woman goes.

It is said that death takes the form of a woman in white who appears walking by the windows or entering the house where someone is about to die. Well known is the legend of the White Lady who would appear in the castle at Jindřichův Hradec when someone from the line of the Lords of Hradec was about to die. In the folklore of the South Slavs, Poles, and Lithuanians, one finds similar personifications of the black death, the *džuma*, or a plague hag. The roots of this lie in the fact that the word "death" in all Slavic languages is of feminine gender. Old Saturn with his scythe or the Christian reaper are not recognized by Slavs as part of their own traditions.

THE PROPHETESS

It should be kept in mind that Czechs have always been keen on prophecies, especially those that involve the Czech lands. The mother of the Přemyslid line, Libuše, is described in Cosmas's Chronicle of the Bohemians as the prophetess of her nation, and the 16th century saw the printing of several books containing prophecies related to the Czech lands, of which two, "The Sibylline Prophecy" and "The Prophecy of a Blind Youth" have been retained in the memory of Czechs, who have accorded them due reverence. In addition, one finds not an insignificant number of minor legends of a more local variety scattered throughout the land, and as they have just as much to say about the future fate of our homeland they might practically be considered prophecies in and of themselves. Many years ago I collected a number of such minor prophetic tales from various localities, and I had in mind to work them into a single poem with the above title. I have never been able to find the time, however, to complete the task, so I give here only six fragments of the intended longer poem. Even so, each could be taken as an integral legend in its own right.

I saw a man on Bělina Voda –

This tale comes from the former Bydžov Region and was first written down by Cosmas and then related by the chronicler Václav Hájek of Libočany, who has it that when Queen Libuše's envoys came to Přemysl of Stadice they found him in the fields, jabbing his oxen with a prick to spur them on in their work. When the envoys had delivered their message, Přemysl stopped what he was doing and shoved the prick into the earth. He untied the oxen and said:

"Go back whence you came!" At which point the oxen elevated, as if they were about to fly off, and then fell beyond the village of Stadice into the cliffs, which immediately closed behind them. The prick of hazel wood that Přemysl had stuck into the earth sprouted three sprigs with green leaves and oblong nuts. While the envoys were sitting with Přemysl, eating bread and drinking water, the plow having been turned upside down with its shares serving as an iron table, they saw two of the sprigs wither and one grow upward. Seeing their astonishment, Přemysl said: "Don't look so surprised! Take it as an omen that my offspring will produce many rulers, but only one will stay to rule your land. And if your lady had not been in such a hurry in this matter, bread would have been abundant for all time: only if I could have finished plowing the field you see before you. But since this work remains unfinished, there will be famine in the land!" – Is it any wonder, then, that these last words would have aroused in the hearts of simple folk the wish: "If only Přemysl would have been able to finish plowing his field!" And this easily could have given rise over time to the legend that a prince will come again to finish this work and thereby bring happiness to the land. This is also oddly associated with the Moravian myth of King Barley [Král Ječmínek], who is awaited as the incarnation of Svatopluk in the hopes that he will usher in a golden age in Moravia. Both of these legends have the same meaning, namely, that good fortune will come only when the cultivation and farming of the land have been thoroughly developed.

I saw Krok's castle in gold
on a rock towering over the river,

This legend is an oral addition to Libuše's well-known prophecy on the founding of Prague and on the coming of St. Václav and St. Vojtěch [St. Wenceslas and St. Adalbert]. It is told that in the vicinity of Vyšehrad Libuše had an enchanted garden, which hung in the air like the gardens of the fabled Queen Semiramis. Beneath the Vyšehrad cliffs, presently the deepest part of the Vltava, was Libuše's favorite place to bathe. It is said that she stood here once on the threshold of her bath, gazing into the streaming water, and foretold from it the coming misfortune for the Czech lands. Unable to change the prophecy, however, she plunged the golden cradle of her first-born son into the water and declared that when it floated to the surface again, then the one who will bring happiness to the Czech lands would be born. The right child would lie in the cradle. So legend has it. – It is generally known that all old Czech chroniclers form the fifteenth century onward considered Charles IV as the savior, on whom they conferred the honorific Father of the Country and during whose reign they say the Czech lands were happy and famed like at no other time before. From this it can be presumed that the promised child of the aforementioned legend,

the salvation of our land . . .

is none other than Holy Roman Emperor Charles IV, which would suggest that this legend's beginnings reach back no earlier than the fifteenth century. Such interpretation is also confirmed by the fact that in the legends of Emperor Charles IV we encounter again and again this cradle, yet transformed into a bed to accommodate the mature age of the subject, as if it had grown with him. I am referring to the legend of the Emperor's miraculous bed at his beloved castle at Karlštejn, on which, as the story goes, no one could lie after Charles's death as the bed would toss out each who tried. In any case, this legend of the golden cradle under Vyšehrad was known to Joseph Hormayr, who published it about thirty years ago.

Above the river Orlice I saw a church

This legend comes from Kostelec nad Orlicí* in the former Hradec Region where the prophesied pine still existed, at least such was the case a few years ago, and it was marked by the many crosses carved into its bark. Evidently, the thrust of this tale is: happiness will come to the Czech lands when its people will all become pious and return to the godly virtues of love, hope, and faith. – "O God, Holy Trinity!" is how one old, early Christian hymn begins.

Don't lament unhappiness, the fate

This legend is told in many places in Bohemia, and the wide variety of versions are dependent on local conditions and the ingenuity of the teller. I once heard it aptly interpreted that this cathedral represents the faith of Christ in Bohemia, and the three gates leading into it the former tripartite creed, whereas the rupture of this faith has been the cause of so much misfortune in the Czech lands. Regardless, there is hardly a more general truism than that feuding and disunity always and everywhere bring misfortune and ruination in their wake. Given our circumstances, these three

---

* Kostelec nad Orlicí is a town in eastern Bohemia near Hradec Králové. Its name literally means Little Church above the Orlice.

gates might be well understood literarily as: Bohemia, Moravia, and Slovakia.

*You who know of the glorious deeds
of your fathers, you like to boast of them:*

If one stands at the corner of the fifth pillar on Prague Bridge [Charles Bridge as of 1870], heading in the direction of Old Town, visible on the Lesser Town side is the remnant of a statue of half a hero jutting up next to the bridge. When whole, the statue portrayed a bearded knight in full armor with raised visor. His right hand rested on a long iron sword, unsheathed, that reached to the level of his beard. His left hand held a shield with the emblem of Old Town, and a lion lay at his feet – the lion and shield can still be seen. The said emblem on the shield was granted to Old Town in 1475 by Emperor Frederick III, which indicates that it was made at a later date. It was in fact a symbol of the right to the bridge, so-called jurisdiction over the bridge, which was bestowed on Old Town by Emperor Charles IV. Local folk have given the statue the name Bruncvík as the lion and sword remind them of the well-known Chronicle of Braunschweig,* which early on was brought into Czech from German, where this mythical knight is many times depicted with lion and sword. During the siege of Prague by the Swedes in 1648, an enemy cannonball knocked off half the statue – the torso with sword – and only the belly and legs with the other recognizable

---

* Bruncvík = Braunschweig / Brunswick. The inspiration for the Bruncvík legend is generally regarded to be Duke Henry the Lion (1130–1195), who made Braunschweig his seat. Yet an alternative view has it originating in Bohemia, not Germany, with Czech rulers as its models.

bits remained, and this is how we see it today.* This surviving lower half has been incorporated into the legend mentioned above in the following sense: it represents the egoism and fatuous superciliousness that currently prevails, and that good will not come until a sincere heart and a sound mind have taken their rightful places.

---

* The present statue was created by Ludvík Šimek in 1884 (thirty years after Erben compiled *A Bouquet*) based on the fragment of the original, which is housed today in the Lapidarium of the National Museum in Prague.

About the Author

Karel Jaromír Erben (Miletín, 1811–Prague, 1870) studied philosophy and law at university in Prague, then worked as a court official and piano teacher before becoming actuary to the Royal Bohemian Learned Society and secretary of the National Museum, at which point he was able to begin collecting folktales and writing poetry. Having achieved the position of archivist of the National Museum and then archivist of the City of Prague, he edited and published important medieval and Renaissance Czech texts. He also collected folk songs, ballads, and tales, and his work includes: *Folk Songs of Bohemia* (1842–45), collecting 500 songs; *Czech Folk Songs and Nursery Rhymes* (1864), a five-volume compendium of Czech folklore; *One Hundred Slavic Folk Tales and Legends in Original Dialects* (1865); and the seminal *Selected Folk Tales and Legends from Other Slavic Branches* (1869). His posthumous *Czech Fairy Tales* comprised his output of prose fiction. *A Bouquet*, published in 1853, is considered his most important contribution to literature.

About the Translator

Translator and poet, Marcela Malek Sulak's work has appeared in a wide variety of literary journals, including *Guernica*, *The Iowa Review*, *Black Warrior Review*, *New Letters*, and *The Cimarron Review*, and she has authored two collections of poetry: *Of All the Things That Don't Exist, I Love You Best* and *Immigrant*. Her translations include K. H. Mácha's *May* (Twisted Spoon Press), and Mutombo Nkulu-N'Sengha's *Bela-Wenda: Voices from the Heart of Africa* (Host Publications). She currently directs the Shaindy Rudoff Graduate Program in Creative Writing at Bar-Ilan University in Israel, where she is Senior Lecturer in the Department of English.

About the Artist

Alén Diviš (1900–1956) was born near the Bohemian town of Poděbrady. Moving to Paris in 1926 to devote himself fully to his art, he came into contact with both French artists and the Czech expatriate community, and he helped to set up the House of Czechoslovak Culture in Paris as a response to the German occupation of Czechoslovakia in 1939. When France fell a year later, Diviš and others from the House were arrested and charged with espionage. He spent the next six months in solitary confinement in La Santé Prison. Though cleared of the charges, Diviš spent another year and a half being shunted through internment camps in France, Morocco, and Martinique before eventually escaping and making his way to New York. His work from this period is often a mix of dark dreams and hallucinatory horror that incorporates the graffiti he remembered from the walls of his prison cell, and it has come to be identified with Art Brut. Diviš returned to Czechoslovakia in 1947 and was starting to achieve some recognition: the publication of his prison memoirs and an exhibition of his art in February 1948. This was also the month the Communist's seized power, and Diviš once again found himself pushed to the margins, destitute and isolated. He went into internal exile and focused on creating artwork to *A Bouquet* and Edgar Allan Poe's short stories. He died in 1956 virtually forgotten, and interest in his work was not revived until after the Communist regime fell in 1989.

Acknowledgments

The publisher would like to thank Tomáš Pospiszyl for helping to select the artwork. Inspiration for this pairing came from the Alén Diviš retrospective he curated with Vanda Skálová in 2005. We are also grateful to Jan Vinduška and Petr Šorm at the Museum of the Elbe Region, Vlastimil Tetiva and Michaela Dobešová at the Aleš South Bohemian Gallery, and Jana Stefanová for graciously allowing us to reproduce work from their collections, and to Oto Palán for providing his photographs of some of the art.

A Bouquet of Czech Folktales by Karel Jaromír Erben is translated by Marcela Malek Sulak from the original Czech *Kytice o pověstí národních*, first published in 1853, expanded to include "Lily" for the second edition in 1861

An earlier version of "Willow" appeared in *Loch Raven Review*

Set in Baskerville Book
All artwork by Alén Diviš
"Author's Notes" translated by Jed Slast

Cover image by Alén Diviš from "Wedding Shirts," courtesy Museum of the Elbe Region

SECOND PRINTING 2020

First published in 2012 by
Twisted Spoon Press
P.O. Box 21, Preslova 12
150 00 Prague 5
Czech Republic

twistedspoonpress@gmail.com
www.twistedspoon.com

Printed in the Czech Republic by Akcent, Vimperk

Distributed to the trade by
Central Books
www.centralbooks.com

SCB Distributors
www.scbdistributors.com